Anonymous

The Question of Hell

an essay in new orthodoxy

Anonymous

The Question of Hell
an essay in new orthodoxy

ISBN/EAN: 9783337387754

Printed in Europe, USA, Canada, Australia, Japan

Cover: Foto ©Andreas Hilbeck / pixelio.de

More available books at **www.hansebooks.com**

QUESTION OF HELL.

An Essay in New Orthodoxy.

BY A PURITAN.

εἴ τις λαλεῖ, ὡς λόγια Θεοῦ·

New Haven:

WILSON & COMPANY.

NEW YORK: AMERICAN NEWS COMPANY.

1873,

Press of DENISON, GRENELL & BARKER,
New Haven, Conn.

ERRATA.

p. 27, line 3 ; for "to that," read "that to."

p. 74, line 3 ; for "AN" read "ON."

p. 76, fifth line from bottom, for "where" read "whence."

p. 81, line 2 ; for "to God" read "of God."

p. 85, line 6 ; for "lasting" read "hasting."

p. 89, line 8; for "sight" read "sigh."

p. 101, lines 1 and 2, belong as lines 2 and 3 on the next page.

p. 102, last line ; for "annointed" read "anointed."

PREFACE.

THE essay here published is intended to break ground in the direction of that new providential interpretation of Christianity which is evidently, and with power and authority, breaking forth from Christian thought and learning and experience, in our age of emancipated and enlightened inquiry. The pages which follow assume the certainty of these three facts,—(1) that Christian confession, in its most unquestioned and thorough types, is in our day undergoing profound regeneration, through the operation evidently of that inward spirit and truth of holiness and love which offer the most indisputable mark of genuine Gospel faith; (2) that, through this regeneration, accredited external orthodoxy—what is called simply "orthodoxy" in the following pages—is giving way to a new, a more profound, and a far more correct orthodoxy ; and (3) that one of the ripest and most evident fruits of this change is the hope, the belief, the courage to implicitly and joyfully trust, that the family of God's moral and spiritual creation is absolutely one through God in Christ reconciling the world unto himself, and that heavenly growth to holiness and blessedness, according to a christening and redeeming power of God working in us, is assured beyond all question, not alone to such as spiritual help reaches effectually in the present initial life, but to those also who fall into the abyss of God's future inexorable punishment of sin, or who through ignorance are all their life here alienated from wisdom and holiness.

That the Divine Kingdom over all souls, revealed in Christ, is one of discipline fully adequate to bring every creature to the stature of a perfect man, its tremendous severities no less than its evident mercies designed in sure wisdom and perfect love, and the Creator's gift, in the very nature of the creature under Divine Fatherhood, a boon of eternal life without exception or repentance, is the solemn, joyful conviction with which the discussion of this little volume has been undertaken. The CHRISTENING FATHERHOOD of God, with its illustration and sacramental symbol in the CHRISTENED HUMANITY of Jesus, to the imitation of which, and heirship of God with which, we are called, would seem to be upon close discrimination, the very truth of Christ for immediate practical use, until we all come in the unity of the faith, and of the knowledge of the Son of God, unto a perfect man, unto the measure of the stature of the fulness of Christ.

That this truth has been no more distinctly and profoundly held, and has only now begun to take the form of loyalty to God and love to man for the redemption unto holiness and heaven of every creature, may be ascribed to this cause—the fact that Disciples' Christianity has always proceeded upon a wrong principle, suggested by the natural and Judaic rather than the regenerate and Christian mind, and has never to any great historical purpose correctly represented the genuine spiritual method of original Christian teaching. Jesus told his own chosen that they must change entirely in order to enter the kingdom in very truth. That he cannot have referred to the conditions of provisional discipleship and personal salvation, is plain upon the face of the matter. He must have referred to the change from very imperfect provisional discipleship, to that complete imitation of himself and thorough discipleship which should make them with him fully sons of God and heirs of the Divine Kingdom. Now this change was never made, at least not in any thorough external way, and in consequence Judaic and natural self-assertion and opinion have thus far ruled the external course of Christian history, and instead of spiritual conformity to Christ, and faith rooted and grounded in the love which he pronounced the true test of real discipleship, there has prevailed a dogma about Jesus, with related dogmas and practices, too often flagrantly false to the divine law of love. Jesus felt constrained to say to an ardent burst of dogmatic devotion in Peter, "Get thee behind me, Satan." It was because the Christ which Peter took him to be was a thoroughly false Christ, inasmuch as it savored of setting up Jesus in a way not consistent with true sacrifice to God. Yet to this day imitation of Peter's zeal in opinion of Jesus has greatly outrun imitation of Christ's pure sacrifice, and for the Gospel ideal of holiness and love, reflected in the obedience of Jesus, we have gospellers' ideas of dogma and ordinance. A discipleship faithfully attempting to obey the repeated and imperative cautions and rebukes aaddressed te the first disciples, to save them from doing as the heathen did and from following false traditions of Judaism, was not attempted by primitive Christianity apart from Paul's single struggle against the older and more immediate apostles, and Paul barely fought down for himself the ban of Petrine orthodoxy, and left no successor to his great task.

But what no Father, no Reformer, no Doctor of the Church, had so much as attempted, universal Christian learning and life have groped towards always, and have unconsciously reached to no small degree within recent years, until it seems only necessary for some clear providential word to be spoken to inaugnrate a reform exceeding in significance everything humanly undertaken on behalf of Christianity since Paul rested from his labors. Such a reform would recur to the Christian discernment which characterized Paul, to divide, in prophetic record, evangelic report, and apostolic teaching, between the very truth of Christ and the intruding leaven of Petrine opinion, and to make definite and thorough and conclusive that evolution of the spirit of holiness and love which has become the prevailing highest mood of Christendom.

It is in the hope that providence and inspiration are indeed bringing about this comprehensive reconsideration of Christian method and matter, and are preparing thereby a new birth of historical Christianity, a regeneration equal to bringing home our faith to awakened mankind, that the present, and some other essays have been prepared, as studies in new orthodoxy. The penman has endeavored to recur to the genuine method of our faith, that of partial and provisional dependence only on text and record, and of a considerable looking unto the unwritten oracles of christened conscience and reason, the lights of that eternal Word which abundantly aids patient search guided by fervent loyalty to God and love to man. And after the manner of this dependence on providence and spirit, he has ventured an appeal of strong confidence to the name and authority of inspiration, as he discerns it in the pure thoughts now deeply moving the Christian mind, and, as of the very truth of God in Christ, has proposed to move the previous question of the Christian Religion —Holiness and Love—upon the dogmatic orthodoxies of sect and creed and church, which have been created after the opinions of men, and not after God in righteousness and true holiness. The essay now published opens a discussion which will be continued in other essays, more specifically devoted to interpreting the essential truth of Christ according to the writer's conception of new, or regenerate and true orthodoxy.

New Haven, Sept. 1st, 1873.

QUESTION OF HELL.

ORTHODOX PERPLEXITY.

There is in our day no more significant theological spectacle than that of the orthodox world with the dogma of eternal punishment in its hands. How not to hold it and how not to drop it, is the problem which drives believers and preachers into all sorts of experimental speculations. It seems as if evangelical faith must break, or at least ease, the yoke of strict orthodox dogma, or perish in the attempt.

THE MISCHIEFS OF UNCERTAIN TEACHING.

The plan of neither holding nor dropping a dogma so conspicuous and significant as that of the eternal perdition of sinners, palsies faith and morality to a perilous degree, neither that nor any other definite view of retribution being distinctly preached to doubting and tempted men. A comprehensive indecision marks the popular pulpit, and to avoid speaking decisively on great topics of sound divinity, preachers resort to the small themes of the passing earthly spectacle, and we hear the catchwords of public gossip instead of the terms of gospel truth. The name of some Jim or Jack of rascality, made notorious by a violent death, runs the round of the pulpits of the land, with an interest keener a great deal than commonly attaches to the name of Jesus. Not that dogmatic views of Jesus are not abundant, nor that everybody would not be greatly shocked at the mere thought of anything conflicting with those views, but simply this, that certain grand aspects of that name, such as that of redemption from eternal misery through it alone, are become so perplexing, if not so doubtful, to average belief, in and out of the pulpit, that very few people want, and very few preachers can give, any distinct, decisive message on such points, and all are content to postpone judgment to come, and find a theme of Sunday interest in the last topic of the day. It may be taken for certain that an overwhelming overthrow of dogma, by the inroad of positive heresy, would be far better than this terribly shaken and doubtful state of the believing mind, and that any energetic attempt to take some ground, clearly and vigorously, with definition and argument, should be heartily welcomed.

AN UNORTHODOX HELL.

In this view of the case, an unusual interest may well attach to a treatise on *The Duration and Nature of Future Punishment*, (by Henry Constable, M. A. Prebendary of Cork), which Prof. C. L. Ives, M. D., of Yale College, has introduced to American readers, in a pamphlet published not long since at New Haven ; especially as Prof. Ives very distinctly and forcibly avows his own conversion to the theory of Mr. Constable, and makes, in a brief introduction, a noteworthy confession and plea, to the most serious prejudice of the current orthodox dogma. As a means of getting a firm and intimate hold of the subject, the more significant statements of these two witnesses are of great value. Both continue to adhere with the most pious sincerity to the absolute authority of Scripture, and both assert a thorough dogma of eternal perdition, at the same time that they destroy root and branch, in their own earnest and carefully reasoned conviction, the old orthodox idea of what perdition is, and do this with an incidental exposure of the interior of orthodoxy, which is alone worthy of the most thoughtful, not to say anxious, attention. If any considerable proportion of orthodox believers are still strict in belief on no better ground than that which Mr. Constable and Prof. Ives appear to have stood upon, we may well expect some great catastrophe to the dogma called orthodox, either a downfall of orthodoxy, or a total change of front, which shall give it the aspect of a new departure, more significant than any which has taken place since Paul turned the infant church out of its judaic nest, adrift over the wide uncertainties of a world of heathenism.

AN. ORTHODOX WITNESS AGAINST ETERNAL HELL.

The confession and plea of the New Haven Professor, which serves as a preface to Mr. Constable's treatise, in the publication to which we have referred, deserves, and will repay, distinct consideration. Professor Ives, though evidently grounded to the fullest measure of piety in dogmatic orthodoxy, and an able and scholarly inquirer, is, as a professor of medicine for the body rather than the soul, a layman in divinity, and on this account somewhat more frank and energetic, as a convert, than an occupant of a pulpit would have been. At any rate he says things which are very much to the point of thorough and candid discussion. To begin with, he remarks upon his own state of mind, while yet professing an orthodox faith, in the following terms :

"Taught from childhood, as doubtless you also have been, that all souls are possessed of immortality, and that, for the wicked ones, hell is a place of eternal torment, I ever accepted the belief, and for years have earnestly enforced it upon others. But, during a recent journey in Europe, my faith in that doctrine was staggered by the sight of the multitudes there and at the thought of the outlying millions still of Asia and Africa, all hurrying on to God's tribunal. Can it be, that in their heedlessness and ignorance, or in their delusive strivings after pardon, they are to meet a doom such as, in its infinity of torture, the human mind could neither conceive nor endure the thought of ? I had learned to know somewhat of the love of God, the Creator and upholder of these lost millions; how could I reconcile that with the accepted doctrine of *unending* suffering? I did try, faithfully; even, in these struggles of the mind, writing home to a doubting Christian brother to confirm him in this belief, which I feared was slipping from under me."

EDUCATION CHIEFLY OCCASIONS THE ORTHODOX FAITH IN HELL.

It appears from this statement, that Dr. Ives is now conscious that education has been the chief occasion of his belief, although that belief has gone to the extent of earnest effort to persuade others. This doubtless is the average ground of a similar belief. Our orthodox Christians accept, insist on, and vigorously contend for, extreme dogmas, chiefly because they have been taught to do so, and find that it is the rule to do so. And by consequence, if ever a large view of the facts of the case is brought home to their minds their belief can hardly fail, having a chiefly traditional foundation, to experience a shock.

DANGER OF REALLY THINKING WHAT HELL MEANS.

Dr. Ives was staggered when he came to really think about it for himself. That he had not before thought about it seems the sole explanation of his previous unshaken confidence that the dogma of eternal perdition is indeed true. A similar failure to really think about it, to comprehend even a little the whole case, is doubtless the explanation of ordinary assent to a dogma so fearful to real thought as that which passes current under the name of eternal punishment. It may be taken almost for granted that no mind fully alive to moral realities ever gave a full assent to this dogma. Either men suppose themselves doing this, while in fact hopes, or at least thoughts, of mercy, are holding them back from full assent, or they give a thorough assent because they are radically selfish and bad, and they think to buy their own security by heartily consenting to promiscuous perdition.

FAITH IN HELL UNNATURAL TO A CHRISTIAN MIND.

To be rooted and grounded in the thought of damnation for others, in the same way that a soul may be rooted and grounded in love, is not possible to a Christian, if indeed it be to anything but a devil. This being the case, it is plain that Dr. Ives is now a witness against his former self, to the effect that, without thinking, and from the effect of education, he held, in Christ's name, a doctrine worthy of the mind of a devil. And this we shall

find both Dr. Ives and Mr. Constable admitting to
have been the case.

INFINITE TORTURE OF SOULS INCREDIBLE.

The great question which rose out of Dr. Ives'
consciousness of the divine love,-like an island
upheaved from the depths of the sea, never to sink
from view again, is a question which no thoroughly
awakened mind can escape—*Is infinite torture of
souls possible to GOD ?* The common disposition
of this question is a verdict of *not proven.* Most
good persons, who think upon the subject, quietly
record this verdict, as one would slyly draw back a
bolt, and there leave the matter. They do not
permit themselves to go a single step further, or
even to admit that they cherish a hope for the
wicked. They innocently disguise, even to themselves, much more in argument with others, their
real hope and trust, by earnestly considering and
urging the reasons why we should *act as if* the
peril of hell were beyond all doubt. In experiences
which make them take definite ground, and compel
them to show where they stand, they let their hope
appear, or even their distinct and firm confidence,
at the same time that they avoid any very open or
thorough denial of the real dead dogma, and do
not venture to profess any very decisive faith that
God rules to redeem. Thus a doctrine of hell,
which is *of hell* in every sense, gets borne on upon

the current of general faith, though no more a part of that faith than a dead log is of the living stream on which it rides to the sea. When education, therefore, shall cease to insist on this dogma, the average Christian mind will be emancipated from it, and faith in redemption, which is now whispered in the ear, will be the open confession of all.

DOGMATIC TEMPTATION TO DISHONESTY.

Dr. Ives tells us that at the very time that his faith was staggered by thoughts which he could not suppress, he tried to act as if no such doubt troubled his own mind. He even avows that he urged a doubting brother not to doubt, at the very moment that he was himself doubting. Such result of a perplexed faith must not surprise us, much less lead us to harsh judgment. It is as honest in the motive as it is otherwise in the act, and we must understand rather than rebuke. But if the very worst trick of mind is not to be accepted as a means of grace, we must energetically put away all such untruth of profession and plea ; earnestly follow light as providence and spirit bring it to our minds, and avoid false confession as a device of the father of lies.

DOGMATIC UNVERACITY.

Dr. Ives did perhaps own to his doubting brother that he also was in doubt, and did not profess, or

imply, a confidence greater than he really had. If
this was not the case, however ; if Dr. Ives, with
his own mind shaken, urged unshaken conviction,
his act was not one whit more moral intrinsically
than any other false sacrifice to God, but was as
thoroughly heathen and superstitious as if it had
been done on the banks of the Ganges, by the most
ignorant of idolaters. We are not bound to confession, much less to argument, of our heart's
faith ; but to attempt either, except in truth and
sincerity, and especially to attempt argument to
which our own confession would give the lie, is
neither praise to God, nor benefit to man, but one
of the greatest delusions and mischiefs possible.

CHRISTIANITY DEMANDS TRUTH OF CONVICTION.

The habit of falsifying real convictions in a supposed duty of standing up for beliefs which are
slipping away from us, is doubtless exceedingly
common. We at least have met it frequently in
our intimate experience of the orthodox religious
world. And it is our deep conviction that nothing
so much as this deserves to be considered against
the rule of Christian faith. That faith places
every soul under the providence and spirit of God,
for every motion of the mind, as well as every act
of life. Careful, therefore, as we may be not to
boldly assume the finger of God in our experience,

we are bound to trust the divine leading of our most earnest efforts to have truth of thought and hope and trust and purpose in the inner man ; and when such efforts bring us to profound questionings ; when they drive the ploughshare of doubt through old faith, to open deeper ground of new faith ; we are bound to study honesty as well as humility, and to no more think of telling, by word or act, what is not true, to a doubting brother, than we would 'tell a lie to the Holy Ghost.

THE CRIME AGAINST CHRIST.

The Christian communion of our day sadly needs open and free confession among its members. Those of our dogmatists who treat such confession as a crime, are sinning with a high hand against the pure doctrine of Christ. They are Jesuits as much worse than the Catholic ever were as the new inquiry of our day is deeper than that which sprang up on Catholic ground. If it please God to decimate, once and again, our orthodox doctors of divinity,* with a plague of sudden summons from this scene of struggling faith, and pour upon them

---

* Such persons will find the story of Ananias and Sapphira a much needed lesson, if they will, in a truthful figure, take the former to represent Catholic Ecclesiasticism, and the latter Protestant dogmatism. The feet of the young men who carried out the former, dead by the hand of God, about the space of three historical hours ago, *are at the door, and shall carry thee out*, thou mother of lies, Protestant Dogmatism !

that remain a spirit of honest opening of their
hearts, that in the fear of God we may all reason
together of the things that concern our peace, it
will be more to the purpose of the coming of the
kingdom of God on earth than anything which has
occurred since Jesus said plainly to a chief apostle,
Get thee behind me, Satan.

LITERAL DEATH IN HELL.

Dr. Ives found in Mr. Constable's treatise on
Future Punishment the doctrine that eternal death
is literally death, the extinction, through the
plague of sin and the pains of hell, of the sinful
soul ; and this he accepted as a substitute for the
orthodox dogma of eternal torment.

ETERNAL EXTINCTION PUT FOR ETERNAL HELL.

The spirit and method of his conversion to this
doctrine of eternal extinction of the wicked, he
indicates in these sentences :

" This view of the future, professedly derived from the
word of God, I carefully and prayerfully compared with the
Scripture record. And there, as I believe, I found it; and so
plainly set forth, I could but wonder that I had so long over
looked it. I had been blinded, as I believe we all are, by the
idea that immortality must be a necessary attribute of every
soul, and so the truth had heretofore lain concealed. But
with the sweeping away of that error, a clearer light is shed
upon the Holy Word itself, which I can now understand as it
was written, not as it is explained for me by commentators.

" Rejecting the traditional dogma of the soul's essential
immortality, denied, it would seem, if anything can be, in the
Bible, our doubts and difficulties vanish with it. The justice

of God, and the question of the origin and end of evil, no longer now need the unsatisfactory explanation of theologic essayists.

"The popular theory that 'every soul is immortal,' is the original lie of our sinful world. It was first uttered in Eden, when Satan declared to our tempted parents—'Ye shall not surely die'; in the same words it is repeated by the Universalist of our day; and it is repeated still, though it be unwittingly and in other words, by every orthodox religious teacher, when he proclaims—'Ye shall live forever in your sins,'. . The arch-deceiver has for centuries persuaded the Christian Church that his lie was not far from the truth. . . Sad that our Protestant forefathers, when they took their stand upon the Bible, and rejected the many errors of a corrupted Church, had not also recognized and rejected this early device of the Old Serpent."

ORTHODOX SOPHISTRY CONTEMNED.

Here again we see that the old view, though firmly held as Bible doctrine, was beset with doubts and difficulties, and that to meet these Dr. Ives had found only "the unsatisfactory explanation of theological essayists." It is a sweeping sentence of contempt against the masters of New England divinity, to brush them aside in this way, as theological essayists; but Dr. Ives is evidently sure of his ground, though it be in high disrespect to Taylor and Dwight, who were masters in New Haven, and to still greater names, with whom has rested the credit of having placed the orthodox system upon a foundation of impregnable reasoning. Prof. Park said in the great Boston Council of Congregationalists a few years since, that an educated man, who was not a Calvinist, was not a respecta-

ble man ; and this rough witticism Dr. Taylor, the
New Haven dogmatist of some years since, who
fills a large place in American theological history,
would have echoed, at least in its spirit. But here
comes a voice from the very camp of Park and Taylor,
a voice that must be deemed at least respectable, to
stigmatize the very key of the orthodox position as
unsatisfactory theological essaying. There is all
the more force in the thrust, from the fact that the
author of it evidently had no purpose to be con-
temptuous. He simply breaks out with fervent
satisfaction at being delivered 'from the cruel mercies of a sophistical dogmatism.

A FALSE USE OF SCRIPTURE CONFESSED.

It is from Bible to Bible, from text to text, nay
from sense to sense within the same texts, that Dr.
Ives has made this journey out of the old into the
new. The spectacle is an instructive one. Dr.
Ives confesses that he has read the Bible with
blinded eyes. He charges this blindness in part
upon the use of commentators ; in part upon
ideas instilled into him from childhood. He has
doubtless avoided heterodox commentators, and
has studiously used such helps as he knew would
confirm his traditional faith. This is the common
course of lay, and even of clerical study, so that
most are in precisely the position which Dr. Ives

says·that he was in until lately ; they read what they believe and believe what they read, and are mere devout parrots of orthodox tradition, no more grounded in thorough intelligence than if mind had been given us to be suppressed, and confession were truest as a service of the lips, irrespective of the motion of the heart.

UNCERTAINTIES OF ORTHODOX INTERPRETATION.

Dr. Ives is now confident that he has heretofore rested in a plainly erroneous and exceedingly perverse interpretation of Scripture. If this be indeed so, who is to assure us that average orthodoxy is not equally plunging into the ditch, not merely as it must be, if Dr. Ives is now right, but on other momentous points of faith ? How does Dr. Ives know that his eyes are even now open to the very truth of God, even on the topic to which his new views relate ?

A mere shifting of the kaleidoscope of texts is alone a very uncertain ground to go upon. Dr. Ives must be aware that even the Mormon delusion is, in its own way, mighty in the Scriptures. He sees, in Mr. Constable's admissions, that the logic of Universalist argument with orthodoxy has been legitimate, if all souls, as orthodoxy assumes, are indeed immortal. Many a hasty disputant, or even wild fanatic, has prayerfully compared his

view with the word of God, and found pegs enough
to hang his notions on. So it is hardly as cheerful for Dr. Ives's readers as for himself, to find how
entirely the aspect of Scripture teaching has
changed in his mind, and how very sure he is that
he was until lately quite blinded by false notions,
and now sees holy writ as it really is.

WHY NOT A STEP FURTHER ?

May it not be that he who lately saw not at all,
now barely sees men as trees walking, and that
another point of view would occasion a further rev-
olution in his belief? It by no means follows that
one touch, even of the hand which is miracle itself,
leaves nothing more to be done. Dr. Ives no longer believes in the eternal torture of souls in hell.
If he were to go and wash in the waters of a purely
spiritual reading of Scripture, he might see the
lost, not as cinders of damnation, but as brands
snatched from the burning, saved as by fire, after
some method worthy at once of perfect justice and
absolute mercy.

A SUSPICIOUS FOUNDATION.

It is a curious circumstance that the turn which
orthodoxy has taken in the convictions of Dr. Ives,
hinges on absolute denial of the great doctrine of
the immortality of the soul. And we must say
that this seems a very suspicious circumstance.

Blinded by this idea of the soul's immortality, are all men, says Dr. Ives. If this were a mere dogma of the creed, and not at once an instinct and a reasoned conviction of natural religion, it would be less difficult to consent to the account which Dr. Ives gives of it.

Or, if we take the other ground, that immortality is a doctrine of special revelation, what is to become of the claim that through Christ this great hope was brought to light ? There has been a grand confidence in the Christain mind because of this claim, and if we are now to learn that this confidence was not just, the situation becomes exceedingly painful. There has seemed to be a divine magnanimity in this beam of light out of eternity, touching with bright promise the head of every creature, and to withdraw this, and say that by nature we were never meant to be any more than the beasts that perish, and that only to such as find Christ does there open any the least prospect of continued existence, seems like a shabby deception. Doubtless theology has been in some respects a shabby deceiver, but this great tenet of human expectation and Christian confidence, has so risen on the world with immeasurable splendor, and has had such a career of inextinguishable brightness through mid heaven, that we reluctantly assist as docile spectators while Dr. Ives and another excellent gentleman show us that the beaming eye of Godhead is only a lantern after all, and to that man as man the path of existence has never known, and never can know, the light of day.

THE OLD SERPENT IN ORTHODOXY.

The terms in which Dr. Ives tenders us his assurance of knowledge on this subject, add to the perplexity with which we listen to him. The idea of immortality he pronounces "the original lie of our sinful world," and this lie he finds in the mouth of "every orthodox religious teacher," disguised a little, but identical with the primal satanic falsehood. The blood of all christendom is poisoned. on this theory, with the virus of the Old Serpent, and where theology has most thought that its work was divinity, it has really blundered into diabolism.

It may be so. The heart of man is unquestionably deceitful, and desperately perverse, in nothing more than in its dogmatic conceits, its raw opinion consecrated by long tradition under the name of religion. The candid scholar, once that his attention is called to the subject, must confess that it is quite possible that some of our most cherished dogmas are really no better than survivals of heathenism, handed down from age to age, in a more and more disguised form, as elements of revelation. But if this is the case, and especially if it has been

the case in respect of one of the great points of
orthodoxy, can we rest so easily as Dr. Ives does in
qualified orthodoxy ? May it not be that the satisfaction with which he reflects on the loss, by extinction, of a large part of mankind, is just as much
from the Old Serpent as the view on that subject
which Christians generally hold ?

FAITH IN HELL BADLY SHAKEN.

' Dr. Ives has some remarks on the condition of
the Christian mind on the question of eternal punishment, which merit a moment's consideration,
before we proceed to the larger field of Mr. Constable's argument. Dr. Ives says :

"A candid, not dogmatic and bitter, review of the grounds
of our belief regarding future punishment is greatly needed
at the present day. I speak for the laymen as one of them,
and I know also, that not a few of our devout and thoughtful
clergymen have serious difficulties on this point Hear this
testimony from that well-known preacher and Bible expos-
itor, Rev. Albert Barnes. Speaking of sin's entrance into the
world, and of that eternity of suffering he felt constrained to
teach, he declares :
"'These are *real*, not imaginary difficulties. . . I confess,
for one, I feel them, and feel them the more sensibly and
powerfully the more I look at them, and the longer I live.
. . I do not know that I have a ray of light on this subject,
which I had not when the subject first flashed across my soul.
I have read, to some extent, what wise and good men have
written. I have looked at their various theories and expla-
nations. I have endeavored to weigh their arguments, for
my whole soul pants for light and relief on these questions.
But I get neither; and in the distress and anguish of my own
spirit, I confess that I see no light whatever. I see not one
ray to disclose to me the reason why sin came into the world ;
why the earth is strewed with the dying and the dead, and

why man must suffer to all eternity. I have never seen a particle of light thrown on these subjects that has given a moment's ease to my tortured mind. . . It is all dark—dark—dark, to my soul, and I cannot disguise it.'

" 'In the midst of this gloom,' as he styles it, Mr. Barnes comforts himself with the belief that, it must be that the Judge of all the earth will do right, though appearances are so much against it; it seeming never to occur to him that his own theology, and not the revealed truth, is here at fault. Others of our religious teachers live on in silence, seeking relief from these felt difficulties in a smothered hope in universal salvation, or at least a final restoration of the wicked, or else they fancy a probation beyond the grave ; in either case failing to give decided utterance of that future woe, so solemnly enforced by the Great Preacher."

NO LIGHT IN ORTHODOXY.

That neither light nor relief are ever found by a deeply thoughtful mind in strict orthodoxy ; that they are very commonly found in a smothered hope of universal salvation, or of final restoration, or at least of a probation beyond the grave ; and that in this state of the case doctrinal teaching has become hesitating and reticent, and almost imbecile, are things which any one may see for himself after some good degree of acquaintance with the movements of the orthodox world.

THE NEW CHRISTIAN HOPE.

About the only thing that discreet and instructed thinkers now pretend to say is that it must be that the Judge of all the earth will do right ; and very few of these can deny that appearances, on the orthodox theory, are anything but right. We may feel pretty sure, therefore, that some great overturning is in preparation, some sweeping round to a new base of the deathless energies of our faith, and that we perhaps who live may be even now hearing the first signals of the greatest change which providence and spirit have yet prepared for Christian mankind.   Let us then with unflinching courage trim and refill the sacred lamp of inquiry after God, and wait with patience for the glorious appearing which is to bring a new heavens and a new earth.

THREE OPINIONS ABOUT HELL.

Mr. Constable's treatise, to which reference has been made, is a very able plea for a peculiar view of eternal punishment.   We propose to follow him through the more striking points of his statement, and to make the course of his argument a point of departure for such suggestions as we desire to offer.   The initial statement of Mr. Constable's position is in the following passage :

"There are three main opinions relative to this punishment.   One of these makes it to be essentially of *a purgative nature*, to be temporary in its duration, and to have as its issue the restoration of all to God's favor and eternal happiness. This was the opinion of Origen.   The second is that which has long been most commonly received.   It makes punishment to be eternal in its duration, and supposes it to consist in *an eternal life* spent in misery and pain.   This was the theory of St. Augustine.   According to the third opinion, punishment is also eternal, but *death*, i. e. *the loss of life*, is its essence, attended and preceded by such various degrees of pain as a just and merciful God, for wise reasons, sees fit to inflict. The third of these opinions is the one here maintained. Its establishment will of course set aside the others. Its eternal duration will overthrow that of Origen ; its character, involving a state of death, will overthrow alike that of Origen and Augustine."—p. 1.

HELL AS PURGATION OF EVIL.

Rearranging for our own purposes the course of the discussion, we will first hear more explicitly in regard to the view here connected with the great name of Origen. Mr. Constable has this to say, in further explanation, and in qualified defence, of this view :

" Origen converts hell into a vast purgatory, and sends men and devils forth from it purified and humbled to the feet of the Great Father and to the joys which are at his right hand forevermore."—p. 59.

" In one grand feature of his theory he commands our entire sympathy. He looked forward to the extinction of evil. His yearning for it was true, was but following out the judgment and reason as well as the longing of every right heart. We cannot look at evil—its hatefulness, its misery, its pollution and think that with such a God as ours this evil will be permitted to extend or to exist forever. So thought Origen, and Scripture bears him out."—p. 63.

" Evil is not to be eternal . . . God has pledged his word and his power that it shall be abolished and destroyed. He has promised a ' *restitution of all th'ngs*' by the mouth of all his holy prophets since the world began."—p. 43.

GOD ETERNALLY AGAINST EVIL.

Here doubtless is the deepest foundation on which faith can build, the thought of God as against all evil forever. If we can tell what this *against all evil forever* should really mean, and

what it should not mean, we solve the problems of
divinity. The great thing, therefore, is to discover
how to keep true to this thought, how to get and
to apply the real meaning of it.

HOW TO BE WITH GOD AGAINST EVIL.

As far as we know, one of the simplest and most
exact rules for this momentous business of keeping
true to God, as the perfection of resistance to evil,
is the old Hebrew rule " To do justly, to love
mercy, and to walk humbly with thy God." If
our concern about justice is practical rather than
speculative ; if from it we proceed to active love of
our fellow-man, after the manner of mercy, which
dictates help, redemption, and good hope ; and if
we bow our heads in simple worship before God,
not attempting to read, much less to judge, his
plan of the government of the universe, we may
expect to find ourselves becoming rooted in a true
faith in God.

ORTHODOX DIVINITY BEGINS EXACTLY WRONG.

This is the exact opposite of the usual method
in divinity. Commonly our teaching puts a slight
upon mere doing justice on our part, and demands
rather that we consider what is the infinite justice,
and its bearing upon our own fate. So far from
being urged to rest in loving mercy, and to make

this the vestibule, as it were, of approach to God, we
are bid take heed to the Divine wrath and our own
selfish need of mercy, and to look out for our own
salvation, and rest not one jot in trying to live for
others. And as for humility as the ground and
rule of our coming to God, we are rather summoned
to inordinate ambition to enter familiarly into a
comprehensive acquaintance with the mind and
ways of Deity, quite as if our salvation depended
on our knowing a fair proportion at least of the
secrets of the universe, and on our taking a hand,
at least by proxy, in keeping up the dignities of
Godhead. This scheme of obsequious attention in the
presence of God, of studying mercy as from God to
ourselves instead of from ourselves to our fellows,
and of slurring righteousness of conduct as " filthy
rags" in the sight of God, exactly reverses the
prophet's rule, on no ground whatever of real
truth.

THE SIMPLEST DUTIES OUR CHIEF CONCERN.

It is both clear reason and evident revelation
that our chief concern is with *our nearest and
simplest duties,* those of common justice, of right
conduct of man with man ; and with that *work of
good will,* of kindness and love, of tenderness of
heart, which has grown more and more upon the
Christian and the human conscience as a divine

task ; and that when we have thus put ourselves to use, and have done with our might whatever our hands find to do, there only remains to us the loyalty of *humble reliance on God*, submission without question or doubt, the submission of penitence, of trust, of unspeakable peace, as becomes children taught by providence and spirit, by law, prophecy, and gospel, to say, simply and sincerely, " Our Father."

SYSTEMATIC DIVINITY A DISTURBER.

So far as systematic divinity has turned men away from this faith and practice of justice, mercy, and humble confidence in God, so far it has done wrong, after the manner, alas ! of human conceit, which is not the manner of grace and truth. The religious world is filled with the noise of loud pretension, the thousand voices of ambition to stand high before God, instead of to walk humbly with him, and mercy and justice are thought no rules at all for redemption, but only incidents of that pride of near approach to God which is miscalled faith.

NO EXCUSE FOR PHARISAIC PRETENSION.

The putting all this upon the name of Jesus makes it no better. To be ready and confident through Jesus in no way excuses the mistake. We may mean to honor Jesus in professing an extensive personal acquaintance with the plans of the

Eternal Mind, and in attaching ourselves familiarly to God, assuming for ourselves a special dignity of peculiar sonship, and we may think we
have great warrant, in Scripture for example, for
doing this, but the solemn fact is that no possible
warrant can justify such departure from simple
humility before God.

HUMILITY BEFORE GOD AN ABSOLUTE DUTY.

Let us hear what we may, or think what we
may, our place remains the same, that of humble
confidence. God is Infinite King and Father ;
and loyalty of trust and love is our absolute, our
eternal, duty. What we can have of this, is our
whole concern ; what we cannot have, we can mend
only by what we have, protesting to God with all
our might our utmost belief, and with our equal
might praying and trusting him to help our unbelief. This is that fear of the Lord which is the
beginning of wisdom, and that faith in God which
is the perfection of wisdom.

FIDELITY BEFORE ORTHODOXY.

It may seem difficult to reconcile Scripture and
Christ with this, but not for that are we warranted
in plunging into the bog of a still greater difficulty,
that in which Dr. Barnes, as we have seen, confesses that he had floundered, without hope or help,
all his days—the difficulty of making our interpre-

tation consistent with the faith and practice of justice, mercy, and humble reliance on God. If we
cannot arrive at both a true fidelity and an orthodox belief, we must defer the latter rather than the
former, until by fidelity we grow up unto faith,
according to the method of coming to know the
doctrine, by doing the will.

Custom is the other way, in consequence of the
perverse conceit with which men take hold of the
matter. But we must be born again from custom
and conceit, in order to reach our place as children
of God, which is not that of exegetes, or dogmatists, or ecclesiastics, but that of humility, of loyalty, of trust, devotion, and obedience.

FILIAL FAITH IMPERATIVE.

The method of thrusting Bible and Christ between the soul and God, and of fixing selfish interest on these, as means of our redemption, has
profoundly disturbed the natural order of religious
experience. No means of grace, no agent of divine
power, no person even of Godhead, can properly cut
off our souls from the Infinite Fount, or rightly
intercept our filial trust.

It is better that we wholly confine our attention
to Jesus teaching his disciples to pray, than that
we permit ourselves to wander from this pattern of

simple dependence on God Our Father, simple submission to him, and childlike trust in his care.

NO REAL NEED OF MUCH DOGMA.

We ought continually to think how apostles
even had to be brought back, as when a little child
was set in their midst to be a lesson to them of the
right method of faith ; and how inevitably the
pride of opinion has carried belief into far too much
dogma, and along paths of questionable and use-
less interpretation.

Suppose that we cannot read the Bible aright
in all its parts, and cannot justly weigh the problems which are become a jungle of theories about
the person of Jesus. We can at least wait on the
spirit and providence of God for guidance in the
matter, and meanwhile attend with all our might
to the simpler, yet not smaller, nor less significant
task, of doing justly, loving mercy, and walking
humbly with God after the instruction of Jesus in
the "Our Father." And if to us so occupied there
come any wild heathen fear that the Father will
murder the children that cry unto him in simple
trust, we can say to such fear, even if it wear the
mask and boast the dignities of a theological system, *Get thee behind me SATAN.*

FAITH IN UNIVERSAL PURIFICATION IS CHRISTIAN.

To apply this view to what Mr. Constable tells

us that Origen taught of the fate of souls, we need but mark the terms of the teaching in question, as these are put by Mr. Constable. It "sends men and Devils forth from purgatorial hell *purified and humbled* to the feet of the Great Father." We omit the mention of "restoration to God's favor and eternal happiness," as not part of the main point of the theory. That point is candidly expressed in the words just quoted ; and we presume no one can question that filial fear of God must rejoice to think of the possibility that all the evil shall be *made good.* It may not be necessary to humble trust in God to assume that this will be so, but such trust can hardly help looking forward to it with very considerable, if not with very strong faith. And the fact actually is, that simple faith in God very commonly grows into a good degree of expectation that all souls will be purified and humbled by all discipline, here or hereafter, and so made true children of God.

DOGMATIC HORROR OF REDEMPTION.

Mr. Constable is very far indeed from having this faith ; for he breathes fury almost against the large hope to which it leads. Thus he says :

"This view would, we firmly believe, if commonly believed, in a single generation reduce the morals of the world to a level with those of Sodom."

Again he says :

" In Origin's view of the future, a view now fast spreading, we see the real cause of the emphatic, repeated, awful declarations of the *eternity* of future punishment. That view, so pleasing to fallen human nature, was the view against which the Spirit of God laid down in Scripture the warnings of everlasting destruction, of unquenchable fire. Experience has proved the necessity of this. Even in the face of these Scriptures men are found to advocate the hope of a restoration from hell. Far more than Augustine's theory does the view here maintained root out this false delusive hope. So long as men believe that life is not extinguished in hell, so long they will nourish hope. They will cherish the idea that somewhere down through the ages, when the groans of hell have been beating sadly, ceaselessly, at the gates of heaven, the message of mercy and deliverance may again be sent down, even as God used to send it of old to Israel groaning beneath the bondage of Egypt, Philistia, and Canaan. Death extirpates all such hopes. 'Corruption has a hope of a kind of removal, but *death has everlasting ruin*,' "—p. 35.

Mr. Constable knows a great deal too much of the purpose and meaning of Scripture. The language "emphatic, repeated, awful declarations of the *eternity* of future punishment," is his own private invention. But if such a text were in Scripture, it would yet become us to pause before it, and by no means to look through it into bottomless horror. Mr. Constable advances a rather crazy opinion when he tells us that faith in the divine recovery of all souls to obedience, would in a single generation reduce the morals of the world to a level with those of Sodom. Frantic exclamation of this sort shows a habit of mind the very opposite to that of faith. To call it infidelity would bc harsh, and yet it has the tone of desperate unbelief.

INFIDELITY OF DOGMA.

What a lack of *faith in man*, to assume that but for the fear of hell we should have Sodom at once !   What frightful *doubt of God's control*, to suppose that it hangs on human opinion on this subject !   But no sane man really has this lack of faith in man and in God.   It is without stopping to think, and out of a wild fervor of mere feeling, that Mr. Constable says that he "firmly believes." It is an orthodox exclamation, not a Christian confession.

NO ASSURANCE OF HELL NEEDED.

Mr. Constable is aware that a hopeful view of future existence is "now fast spreading."   He admits that " men are found to advocate a restoration from hell."   Indeed, he candidly avows that this must be so ; that, so long as the lost continue to exist, some one will nourish hope for them.   And he claims it as a grand merit of his theory that it cuts off such trusting hope, as no other theory does.   Here again he runs before he is sent.   The children of God do not require insurance against the redemption of the lost.

AN INFINITE OPEN HOPE.

On the contrary, they do require *an infinite open*

hope. They may fear the worst on many grounds, and may really hope and believe only where their affections are engaged, or after they have reached a profound knowledge of faith working by love, but in no case do they require, or should they permit, hope to be closed and trust to be cut off. When, therefore, Mr. Constable, or any other dogmatist, undertakes to put *everlasting ruin* at the end of faith's prospect of the destiny of all souls, he does exactly the wrong thing. If the books of hope are ever closed, it will be by no hand other than that of *final* divine purpose. Anticipation of that purpose is contrary to the law of Christian faith.

DOGMATIC RAGE.

Origen's handling of Scripture excites the ire and scorn of Mr. Constable, as the following sentences will show :

" Origen never found any difficulty in Scripture. If it was for him, well and good If it was against him, he made it without any ceremony speak as he wished."

" Every reader of Scripture knows that its solemn warnings are addressed *to the sinner in person :* ' *O wicked man, thou shalt surely die.*' Death, Destruction, Perdition, Loss of Life —all the multiplied phrases and illustrations of the Bible are there directed against *the persons* of the wicked. Origen's simple mode of neutralizing their force is by directing them *against their sin* And so his point is gained. Their force cannot be too strong for him, so he does not attempt to diminish it. The Augustinian, directing them against the sinner, robs them of their meaning : Origen directing them against the sin, leaves them their proper sense. Both pervert

Scripture, and it is difficult to say against which the charge is the heaviest.

We meet with Origen's free and easy method of Scripture everywhere throughout his writings. Whatever be our opinion of Origen personally, of his learning, his brilliancy, even of the truth of much of his teaching, his teaching here places him among those prophets condemned by Ezekiel for 'strengthening the hands of the wicked, that he should not return from his wicked way, *by promising him life.*"—p. 62.

INADVERTENT FALSEHOOD.

The last word of this quotation is one of those inadvertent untruths which crowd the history of theological controversy. Neither Origen, nor Origen's hopeful theory, aim in the slightest degree to strengthen the hands of the wicked, that he should not return from his wicked way. The sole aim of this theory is to strengthen right, and bring man back to God. To threaten severe, sin-crushing discipline, with the minatory promise that it will be insisted on to the bitter end, and made as effectual as the very furnace of fire is to gold in the refiner's hands, is the exact opposite of giving aid and comfort to the wicked.

PURGATION THE TRUE SEVERITY.

The reaction against violent orthodoxy has perhaps worn an appearance of getting the sinner off, of rescuing him from penalty, of breaking down the tremendous severities of discipline, but this is no part of a wise hope in the redemptive efficacy of the divine justice. On the contrary, such a hope, held with humility not less than confidence, affords the best possible ground on which to build a thorough, irresistible doctrine of the divine severity against sin. It has no appearance of injustice, yet lacks no rigor of infinite regard for law, since it at once asserts law effectually over all the disobedient, and makes this assertion a perfect moral benefit to the sufferer, as well as to creature society in general. If searching rebuke of sin is to come back to our pulpits, it must be when the stroke of severity is at once weighted and steadied by the certainty that we may justly have good hope of the perfect, the universal and absolute, *efficiency* of the divine discipline.

ETERNAL DEATH TO SIN.

It is wholly untrue, then, that hope promises life to the wicked, that he should not return from his wicked way. It promises death rather, and a death more significant and effectual than extinction. Our spirits can resist torment, especially when we distinctly anticipate a final end of pain. Milton obeyed a just instinct in making the courage and greatness of Satan more than a match, in a moral point of view, for the wrath of Jehovah. It is a petty and vulgar justice which deals in vindictive torment, and against such a justice even the breast of mortal man is triply armed. And if such a justice proposes to kill as well as to injure, it is not very difficult for the creature to accept the chance, and make the most of *its defeat of God.* It will at least have an end, extinction, and he that tortures and kills will make nothing out of it, unless it be a pleasure in working torment, which hardly a devil would be so devilish as to take.

But death to desires, to purposes, to that in our very nature which works evil, is a visitation worthy the name of death. Not only is it a death which avenges law upon us and in us, but it is a death which steals upon our false choice, our wrong will, our darkened thought, with terrors whose hue is indeed that of eternity.

NOT THE TEXTS BUT THE FAITH.

Mr. Constable thinks it a free and easy method which the advocate of hope uses in his handling of Scripture. It may be so, but it is at least the method of faith. We are not required to digest the promiscuous letter of Scripture. On the contrary, we are free to take and eat as we can, accordinging to our faith, never going against faith merely to swallow a text. Some of us may understand much, and some of us may understand very little, of Scripture ; that does not so much matter, if, so far as we go, we keep the rule of faith.

IN SPIRIT AND TRUTH.

We cannot keep two rules at once ; we cannot serve the spirit and yet be slaves to the letter. · If we bind ourselves to the letter then we must stand largely free from the spirit ; while if we bind ourselves to the spirit we must stand largely free from the texts, until we learn how to see the spirit in them. Common orthodox service is in the letter, but the truer Christian service is in spirit and in truth. So it must be easy for faith to evade the text, not by denial, but by patient expectation of a new light in it. And Christianity especially secures to us the fullest freedom to confine our worship to spirit and truth in the inner man. Dogmatists who thrust upon us either this mountain or that, offend against the distinctive character of Christian doctrine. To all their systems faith says, "Be ye taken up, and be ye cast into the depths of the sea," *and it shall be done.*

ORTHODOXY A HUMAN INVENTION.

Mr. Constable is unsparing in his criticism of the way in which the current orthodoxy makes out its case. One of his exclamatory statements, intrinsically worthless as it is, will yet serve as a suggestion to our reflections upon the intellectual condition of the average orthodox mind. It is as follows :

"Ah ! may we not well enquire whether the Church of to-day is not, like the Pharisees of old, 'teaching for doctrines the commandments of men ?' "

As Mr. Constable makes this enquiry, it amounts only to an exaggerated expression of his hostility to hell with a *dum* rather than hell with a *dee*. In itself, however, and on broad general grounds, the question is one which forces itself upon Christian attention. The long career of orthodoxy, Catholic or Protestant, has borne fruits which compel faith to precisely this inquiry, whether men have not put their own notions in place of the divine word ? And taking the verdict of each class of believers separately, we find the opinion universal that this has been done.

HEADY HUMAN OPINION.

No sect accuses itself, but every one accuses another, with a degree of judgment which is itself manifestly contrary to faith. The Catholics exclude all Protestants, as no better than aliens and infidels, and support their exclusion by a majority vote of Christendom. The Protestants in their turn exclude the Catholics, and sustain their judgment by the undoubted weight of the more intelligent class of believers. Among Protestants every sect without exception lies under the ban of other sects on some grave point of faith and practice, to the extent of actually being voted down by a majority of Protestants on the point or points which it individually cherishes.

Thus it is the common charge everywhere that human notions have intruded upon divine truth. And the spirit of this charge is, to a very large extent, a spirit of anxious superstition, of intense self-will, no more Christian than a similar spirit among heathen. Men act as if they were afraid God would kill them if they exercised charity, and they push their objections to their brethren with a heat which has far more assertion of will in it than love of truth, of man, or of God.

BAD REPUTE OF ORTHODOXY.

The brand on all the theologies of Christendom is "*odium theologicum;*" the just reflection of mankind is, " How these dogmatists hate one another ! " And with such an appearance it is fair to presume that there has been, to some degree, and however unwittingly and innocently, a comprehensive "teaching for doctrines the commandments of men."

" Beware of the leaven of the Pharisees," and " Get thee behind me," and similar short and sharp methods with the tendency to this very mistake, were necessary in the beginning, and seem not less necessary now. Nor can it surprise us, when we reflect how nearly impossible simplicity of allegiance, by justice, and mercy, and humble trust, is, and how natural it is to want some great place, even of penitence and humility, and some conspicuous ground and lofty standing, even though it be for shame and punishment, or for redemption by rescue out of the very burnings of wrath.

ORTHODOX LOUDNESS AND DIVINE SILENCE.

The dogmatic mind swells with a sense of the spectacular importance of sin, and punishment, and atonement, and sniffs at the thought of a silent operation of God with his creatures, and of a quiet return of the soul to holiness and heaven. It is not in any of the great theologies that the spirit bloweth as it listeth, or that God comes to the heart of man with still small voice. Neither Catholicism, nor Calvinism, nor Methodism, nor Unitarianism, will ever have it said of its meaning, "Thou canst not tell whence it cometh nor whither it goeth." If there were not a Christianity which doth not cry in the creeds, and a Christ whose voice is not heard in the proof texts, and a power of God working in us above all that we ask or profess, all that we think or pretend, it would be to little purpose to prefer the Christian name to a heathen, or to imagine that religion has enduring and redeeming power.

SURVIVAL OF HEATHEN METHOD AND FAITH.

On very broad grounds, then, we think it very
pertinent to inquire " whether the church of to-
day is not, like the Pharisees of old, ' teaching for
doctrines the commandments of men ;' " and of
heathen men at that. The result of such an inquiry would bear very materially upon the solution
of the problems brought before us in Mr. Constable's pamphlet, since it seems highly probable that
the blackness of darkness which rests upon the orthodox solution of those problems, is directly due
to a survival of heathen methods and beliefs, and
since also we may reasonably surmise that even
Mr. Constable's variation of the doctrine of perdition has no warrant beyond the same shadow of
heathen terror and heathen opinion.

FEEBLE WITNESS OF BIBLE TO HELL.

Mr. Constable takes in hand the orthodox appeal to the Bible, with as little reserve as if he had
not lately held an orthodox view himself. It
would be interesting to know how commonly
preachers of the eternity of future misery meet
the difficulty described in the following :

"Has it never occurred to the reader, as to myself, when
searching for biblical language in which to present and en-
force the eternity of future suffering, to be surprised and
puzzled to observe how unsatisfactory and feeble seem all the
Apostolic references to future unending woe ? "

THE BIBLE DOES NOT CUT OFF HOPE.

Mr. Constable catches but a glimpse of a very large and very significant fact, enough for his small purpose of shifting the stage scenery of hell, but not enough for securing a just view of the momentous topic under discussion. That fact is that we have no firm ground in either evangelist or apostle for cutting off the operation of Christian faith, in the case of the lost, and hence are not warranted in doing this.

NO DEMONSTRATION OF HELL.

Faith issues in hope at least, if not in trust, or even in the perfect love whose covenant cannot be broken, and only the strongest demonstration could stop this action of faith. Such demonstration does not exist. Whatever does exist is simply matter for reserved inquiry, without perplexity, least of all doubt and despair. If we cannot dispose of it we can at least let it alone, and go about the business of faith, trusting that by doing what is practical we shall in due time wholly understand.

The case which Mr. Constable finds feeble and unsatisfactory, was never meant to be anything else, and even the case which Mr. Constable sticks in, that of his own idea of hell, would seem no less weak and unimportant, if due heed were paid to the point of view of pure and simple faith.

A "BASELESS AND HORRID CREED."

It is easy for Mr. Constable to see how foolishly the orthodox mind falls into the ditch of a "baseless and horrid creed." For example, the following are some of his sentences :

"The ordinary Greek Lexicon, not lexicons of the New Testament, colored and tainted by theological opinion, is the true guide to the Greek of the New Testament.—p. 14. . . . . Dictionaries of the New Testament, and commentators on it, may, if they please, put upon the phrase the sense of '*happiness*' in the numberless passages where it occurs, but we deny to them the right to alter the meaning of a well understood Grecian word for the sake of bolstering up their baseless and horrid creed.—p. 16. . . . . . That is what the holders of Augustine's theory have done. They put an insufficient, and inapposite, an unnatural, or a positively false meaning on the most important terms of the New Testament. With them death means life, and life means happiness, and so on. Having put these convenient meanings on the phraseology of Scripture, interpreted as they would not dare to interpret the code of a human legislator, they can look placidly on a thousand passages which contradict what they teach from platform, and pulpit, and press, and instil into children's minds almost with their mother's milk."—p. 59.

"We now come to the famous passages in the Book of Revelation. Driven hopelessly from the plainer parts of Scripture, the advocates of eternal life in hell think that they have in this obscure, mysterious, and highly-wrought figurative book, at least two passages which authorize them to change numberless passages in the rest of Scripture, and some even in the Book of Revelation itself, from their plain and obvious meaning to one that is forced, unnatural, and often false to all the laws of the interpretation of language."—p. 30.

HOW TO BOLSTER UP HEATHENISM.

If Mr. Constable unwittingly held, or deliberately held, not long since, a baseless and horrid theological opinion ; if he did this by altering the meaning of well understood words, and by putting a positively false meaning on most important proof-texts ; if he dared to interpret the Bible any way and every way to suit the exigencies of a heathen dogma,—and all this he brings against his recent self and his orthodox brethren,—we may well assume that the method which leads to such results is a very doubtful one.

THE SACRIFICE OF TRUTH AND RIGHT.

Our own observation had prepared us for Mr. Constable's confession of orthodox want of veracity and exegetical rectitude. It seems quite right to the orthodox mind to accept as from God a horrid opinion, however baseless simple faith may find it. The idea is that by so doing the mind makes a suitable sacrifice to God. And who is to tell the deluded worshipper, that every such sacrifice is essentially heathen.

SERVING GOD WITH LYING LIPS.

The heathen habit of mind, panic fear before God, and the heathen opinion, that God demands the flow of blood, figurative if not literal, some sacrifice of the best, remain in full vigor with the average orthodox pietist. And with God looking on to damn him if he flinch or fail, why should he not hustle texts into any convenient form, regard-less of their individual significance, and only at-tentive to the exigencies of his sacrifice ? Is a man to heed the probable individual purpose of a verse of Scripture, when, if he should be misguided by evident appearances, he may have to go to hell for his blunder ? Is he not more likely, under the influence of fear and of concern for self, to make a *safe* use of a text, rather than an apparently true one ? What is the appearance of truth but that reflection of reason which superstition delights to sacrifice ? The common plea to this day of aver-age orthodoxy is that we should bow reason to God, and that it is *safest* to see God in the dogma which Mr. Constable has found courage to call baseless and horrid.

HOPELESS DISHONESTY OF ORTHODOXY.

So long therefore as concern for safety is the first motive to religion, and the opinion that God is pleased with anything but truth and right holds full sway, so long will pietists twist evident facts to support horrid opinions. Mr. Constable him-self is not yet out of the meshes of this false and selfish method.

THE PRACTICAL FAILURE OF HELL.

The practical failure of the doctrine of hell is sketched by Mr. Constable in the following terms :

" It has often been remarked that where a punishment felt to be excessive is threatened,—it wholly fails of its effect. The criminal is satisfied that it will not be executed. It is thus with the theory of everlasting misery as a punishment for human sin. *It is practically disbelieved.* The sinner takes refuge from it in a thousand ways. The greater portion of the professing Christian Church has adopted purgatory as an escape for them from this hell. Even for those who cannot accept a purgatory the vulgar notion of hell has no practical terrors. Even if they do not reject it altogether as a mere bugbear, they do not believe in it *for themselves.* A change of life, a word of penitence at the last, a sigh of sorrow for the past as the soul is leaving its tabernacle, will surely avert *from them* a fate too terrible for a merciful God to inflict And so the very transcendent terrors of the vulgar hell defeat the object of threatened penalty, for few, if any, believe in its infliction *on themselves.*"—p, 64.

FAITH CASTS OUT FEAR.

It is a significant illustration of the doom of the dogmatist to blindness of mind, that Mr. Constable does not see that every word of this tells just as forcibly against one sort of eternal perdition as another. Does Mr. Constable suppose that "the greater portion of the Christian Church" will be so pleased at the idea of burning people all up in hell, as to give up a hope of purgatorial discipline, and that too when this hope is in the strictest analogy with simple faith? Or is it to be presumed that the great mass of unbelievers, who put aside the common idea of hell, on various grounds, will not just as readily evade any other idea of terrible damnation? It does not rob perdition of all its terrors to make it a death of the soul after a season

of torment. This also is too incredible to be practically believed by any one who would not believe
the orthodox notion. Timid pietists will creep
away from the shadow of either terror ; venture-
some doubt will face either exactly alike ; while
clear faith knows no more of the one horror than of
the other.

ORTHODOX TEACHING STIGMATIZED.

Mr. Constable uses great vigor and courage in
his denial of the orthodox theory of hell. He
says : "We abhor Augustine's theory." He
speaks of the arguments used in its support as
"arguments which we feel unworthy of a child."
The course which it ascribes to God he denounces
as a "procedure which our heart whispers to us
is only worthy of hell." He stigmatizes the orthodox teaching of Augustine on the subject as
"Semi-Manichaeism," and pronounces it "at direct issue with the authority of Scripture." He
declares that "the theory of eternal life in hell
contradicts the whole tenor of the Bible." Speaking of those who "sinned without law," he says
that "Augustine's sentence against such is one of
the blackest tyranny and injustice." The idea
that all souls are immortal has, he asserts, "led
good men, under the specious pretext of exhibiting the Divine justice and holiness as infinite, to

paint God as a monster of unutterable cruelty."

A SPECIOUS PRETEXT.

For a confession from the bosom of orthodoxy this is surprisingly exact. The last sentence just quoted touches the quick of the orthodox argument. The plea for hell in orthodox dogmatism is indeed based on the "specious pretext of exhibiting the Divine justice and holiness." It is a mere pretext. No man, directly anxious to honor the justice and holiness of God, will turn his mind to the damnation of other people as a means thereto. He may leave himself in the hands of God, for better or for worse ; and he will do so rather than make it his first business to find some means of escape from the Divine discipline.

SIMPLE SUBMISSION ALONE HONORS GOD.

If the soul awakened to desire the glory of God, and moved to faith in him, seems to itself worthy of hell, it will say so submissively, and leave the matter entirely to God. If redemption comes to such a soul, it will come of the free grace of God, not through any scheme of begging off and paying up and getting quit, either with or without intervention of a second party. To set the soul upon pushing its part in any such scheme, as if loyalty to God could be shown by concern

for one's own safety, and it were honor enough to
God to let us off, on the basis of a good scheme, is
absurdly contrary to a just idea of regard for the
character of Deity. If we honestly desire honor
to the Divine justice and holiness, we have no
choice but to submit ourselves absolutely, trusting
that God cannot do wrong, not even to a sinner,
and willing that he should do right, though he
slay us.

THE ORTHODOX SCHEME NO HONOR TO GOD.

The theory, therefore, which affects to honor
God by according to him the right to inflict the
pains of hell, provided that we may in good time
dodge the infliction, has no rectitude or veracity in
it ; it is a trick of human conceit and selfishness,
as mere a pretext as ever superstition suggested to
the mind of man. Any sincere mind, once brought
round from the orthodox to the Christian point of
view, from selfish fear to unselfish faith, will see
this without difficulty. It is remarkable that Mr.
Constable should see it while still holding on to a
modified orthodoxy.

A PEDIGREE OF DISHONOR.

In disposing of the orthodox dogma of hell,
Mr. Constable looks up its historical appearance
On this point he remarks :

"The first known holder of the theory of eternal life for the reprobate was the author of the writings known under the title of 'Clementina,' and falsely attributed to Clemens Romanus. . . . . This nameless forger is, so far as is known, the first maintainer of the doctrine of eternal life in hell. . . Here in these shameless forgeries, and these vagaries of unhallowed fancy, lies the mean origin of a dogma which *now overshadows* the Christian Church.

"UNHALLOWED" AND "SHAMELESS."

We need not pause to weigh the historical value of this statement. It is sufficient to consider its significance as a confession. The author of it is in full sympathy with the dogmatic system of orthodoxy, except on the one point of the duration and nature of future punishment. He rests his faith on Scripture alone, and he shrinks with horror from any really liberal conception of dealing with sin. In fact he thinks his notion of hell more terribly effective than any other. He thinks that he believes that we should have universal Sodom within one generation if the fear of hell were removed. There is no liberal taint in his pietism. He has simply hit upon a particular interpretation of sacred texts, and he pushes this with precisely the average dogmatic spirit. As near as possible, therefore. he is a witness from the midst of orthodoxy. And the ability, dignity, and learning with which he writes, assure us that he is more than a common witness. When then he

tells us that vagaries of unhallowed fancy, disguised in shameless forgeries, were the origin of a
doctrine which now overshadows, and which for
more than fifteen hundred years has overshadowed,
the Christian Church, we may very properly regard so damaging a statement as a grave additional
reason for pushing from us the whole structure of
orthodox dogmatism, and for resting in the simple
faith and practice of Christian principles. The
mere possibility that such a thing has happened,
through excess of human opinion in Christian theology, should send us back to the simplest faith.

THE SHAME UNDENIABLE.

We are born under a vast dogmatic system ; education and custom press it upon us ; persuasion
and persecution hold us back from going out of it ;
and, behold, a credible witness, who has no hostile
motive, who wishes only a slight readjustment of a
single conception, breaks out with the declaration
that the conception which he wishes to displace
was the invention of unhallowed fancy, and was
originally palmed upon the church by a shameless
forger. Can an indignant church reply, not
merely that it was not so in this case, but that it
could not have been so ? Alas for a Church which
certainly cannot so reply, and to which no candid
scholar can give credit in such a matter without go-

ing into court, and hearing unquestioned evidence. And when all the evidence is heard, we fear that it will only show to what an enormous extent the authoritative dogmas of Christendom are an intrusion and a fraud upon Christian faith.

HORRID FEATURES OF THE DOGMA OF HELL.

That Mr. Constable, once able to stand back from the dogma of eternal torture of souls, and to take in all its hideous aspects, regards it as an outrage upon every humane and godly instinct of rational man, is made very plain in the following vigorous statement :

"What is our question ? It is this. Is pain, inflicted through eternity, endured without any hope of an end, no nearer to its close when numberless cycles have passed than when the first groan was uttered,—is such *a just punishment* for any conceivable amount of sin committed by the worst of men ? Man did not ask for life : it was given him without his knowledge or consent. Can any abuse of this unasked-for gift justify the recompense of an existence spent in unending agony ?

" We must put the question on its proper grounds. The ablest modern defenders of eternal life in hell have put it on a false issue. They have done so in two main respects, urged on by their inability to justify their theory in its naked light. The first of these we will give in the words of William Archer Butler, whose view is adopted by Dr. Salmon, Professor Mansel, and others. ' *The punishments of hell,*' says Butler, ' are but the perpetual vengeance that accompanies *the sins of hell*, An eternity of wickedness brings with it an eternity of woe. The sinner is to suffer for everlasting, *but it is because the sin itself is as everlasting as the suffering.*'

"It may fairly be questioned whether, according to any principles of Divine or human law, the lost in hell are *capable of sinning*. We do not believe they are. Out of and beyond all

law, they are incapable of transgressing law. But independ-
ently of this, it is sufficient to say of the above fearful view
that it contradicts the Scriptures. Not once or twice, but
over and over again, it tells us that *the punishment of the future
is for the sins of the present times.* If we think it too great, we
are not at liberty to throw in the sins of the future, real or
imaginary, to justify the punishment of the future. If we
cannot defend man's future treatment as being a just award
for his present conduct, we cannot justify it at all. It is a
piece of the coolest effrontery for us to present as a reason
for God's conduct what God has not Himself presented when
explaining to man His judicial conduct. Just fancy an earthly
judge sentencing a criminal to a punishment too severe for the
offense committed, and then gravely justifying his sentence
by the observation that the criminal *would be sure to deserve it
all by his conduct in gaol!* Yet such is the judicature, unworthy of a Jeffreys, which learned professors of theology and
doctors of divinity ascribe to the Judge of the whole earth!

"Nor does it relieve God in the smallest measure from the
charge of injustice to say that future punishment will but
follow that law of nature which inextricably links together
sin and misery. The laws of nature are the laws of God.
For all their consequences, after they have worked their uni-
form work for ages, He is just as responsible as when He first
ordained them, or as when He departs from them by an alter-
ation of law or a miraculous interference. So Bishop Butler
argues in the place above referred to. If the laws of nature
were to bring on the sinner a punishment greater than his
sin deserved, it is God Himself who would be doing so.

"The simple question then is, could man by any conduct
here deserve to suffer throughout eternity pain and torment
to which only the worst pain he suffers here can afford a true
parallel? Would the agonies to which the martyr was sub-
jected for an hour be only sufficient for the sinner if drawn
out through the eternal age? Would it be just in God to inflict this on any single creature of his hand, on any being
who would never have had life at all if the Maker had not
called him from his clay? The verdict of the human heart
—in its fierce denial—in its secret recoil—answers No.
'Eternal pain,' says Augustine, 'seems harsh and unjust to
human sense.' 'With the majority of men of the world,'
says Butler, 'this doctrine seems, when they think at all about
it, monstrous, disproportioned, impossible.' It seems so, in
the same writer's mind, to others besides men of the world,'

to men who do not fear this doom for themselves ; 'it would blanch the intellect,' reduce the mind of the Christian to a state of idiotcy, deprive him of life, were he but ' adequately to conceive it.' If God were now to ask man whether his conduct on this hypothesis were just, man would with one voice reply that it was not.

"The history of human religious thought shows man's ineradicable sense of the burning wrong of this fearful theory. If Plato, deriving his inspiration from Egypt, taught a Tartarus with its fiery streams whence none could come forth, he taught it for an infinitesimally small portion of men. For most—even for the homicide, the parricide, and the matricide—he had his Acherusian Lake, whence, after a purgative process, they issued forth again to the upper air. If Augustine adopted his great master's abode of unending pain, he adopted also his purgatory, from whence there was a way to heaven. If the Church of Rome has sanctioned the theory of Augustine, she practically holds out its terrors only to those without her pale of safety : for her own millions she has, at the worst, the fires of a finite period. The assertion of Augustine's hell did but drive the gentler mind of Origen to the notion of a wider purgatory than Rome's or Augustine's, where even devils should be prepared to resume their place in heaven. The Churches of the Reformation have generally followed Augustine in his hell and denied his purgatory, but at all times within their bosom has been a struggle against the dominant doctrine, and, even from those who maintained it, it has generally commanded only a sullen, uncheerful assent. Such men as Tillotson, Robert Hall, Isaak Taylor, Albert Barnes, while they accepted the theory, loved it not. We constantly find its recent defenders candidly confessing that with all their heart they would wish that it was a lie. The modern mind, shaken in religious faith, denies the inspiration of a book which is supposed to teach the monstrous creed. With those who will not throw away their faith in man's future, the theory of Origen, with all its consequences, bids fair, if only confronted with the fearful nightmare of Augustine, to take the place which the authority of the latter father has given to his views. The modern defenders of Augustine's theory shrink from putting forward a vindication of it in its plain and hideous aspect. One after another of the arguments on which it has heretofore been defended they have abandoned as unworthy of their reason, or abhorrent to their sense of justice."

"Hell is not the eternal abode of evil, concentrated in intensity, deepening and darkening in hue throughout eternity. It is not the everlasting exhibition of a scene with whose moral horrors all the sensuality, and deviltry, and hate, and despair that has been exhibited in earth's foulest dens could not compare. . . . Thank God, it is not true. God does not contemplate *this* hell.

"The hell of Scripture is the very counterpart to that fearful scene which Augustine has depicted. The very thought of this latter is too horrible to think. However ancient, it is no part of 'the faith once delivered to the saints.' We therefore reject it as a fable, a novelty, a monstrous doctrine worthy of the Koran, where it takes its fitting place—unworthy of the Gospel, where it finds no place. We leave it to the disciple of Mohammed, lying on his couch of sensuality, to look down with cruel delight upon a scene of unutterable and endless misery. This is not the consummation which the disciples of Christ, or the worshippers of the Father of mercies are called on to rejoice in. They could not look on it and rejoice ; they could not regard pain as endless without feeling that unalloyed joy could never be their own."—pp. 65, 66.

HELL A MORAL HORROR.

It is quite just to leave the expectation of hell to the most utterly sensual, or the most thoroughly selfish of moral creatures. The dogma belongs in the lowest and basest types of religion. No decently moral nature can contemplate the merest chance of such a gathering into one of vile energies and detestable horrors without feeling unutterably moved to resist it, to overcome it, to suppress and exterminate it. People may well be shy of arguing for hell in clear and cool reason, apart from the heat of dogmatism, or the blindness of superstition. Undoubtedly the mere progress of virtue, the most ordinary experience of elevation of character, is blotting out faith in the plague of eternal woe, and preparing the way of a distinctly contrary doctrine. There is no authority which can long stand up against this irrepressible moral advance of Christian mankind. If the Bible teaches the dogma of hell, faith will be thereby convinced that it is not the book which is divine, but the word of holy truth which the book may prove to contain. An inveterate divinity in every good man's heart forbids, as with the voice of indwelling God, the admission of the hateful doctrine into the holier place of the heart, where love dwelleth ; nay more than this, decent human instinct keeps it, like a leper, at a distance. The more souls grow into the likeness of God, the more they grow away from this looking for of poison and fire and all hell torment.

THE PROTESTANT DOGMA WORSE THAN THE CATHOLIC.

It is something astonishing that the Protestant dogma should be so much harder and blacker than the Catholic. Perhaps it is chiefly due to the fact that Protestantism is really a bolder departure from living inspiration than Catholicism is. The latter possesses a respectable faith in the presence of deity in a general communion of mankind, though it falsely limits this communion to her own mankind. Protestantism is a long way more exclusive and Pharisaic than the older form of church and creed. She thanks God that none of her children are as other men are, while Rome uses the Christian rule far more thoroughly, and receives into her fold, not those who are already Christian, but all who are willing to come to her to be made Christian. If God does as well by his children as Rome by hers, then is no soul shut out from hope.

BOTTOMLESS EVIL IMPOSSIBLE IN A MORAL UNIVERSE.

This is a true paternal as well as maternal instinct, to hold on to all, with courage and hope to recover all. The purging away of evil belongs in a just conception of discipline. No philosophy of the universe is so much as respectable which does not lend to divine law this disciplinary efficacy. Right and wrong would cease to mean anything if we should once really apprehend a tide of uncontrolled wrong setting forever towards a gulf of bottomless evil. Right is the way the divine law makes things go, and if it makes things go wrong, then is wrong right, and our philosophy is crazy. Crazy! It would be hell itself to really know of hell, or adequately to conceive the horrors of perdition.

A THEOLOGICAL WHOPPER.

God speaks conclusively in the breast of man to give the lie direct to all assertion of horrible torture in the universe. If such were the effect of Godhead working through natural law, then were it better that unpitying force be our mother, for this at least is not positively malignant, does not poison the wound as well as crush. Earth has never seen judgment such as the orthodox dogma ascribes to God ; to speak of it as based in justice, this exceeding weight of horrible injury, which will never let up to all eternity, is truly a theological whopper.

A WICKED PROPHECY.

No wonder that the dogmatists are anxious to turn prophets, and to tell us what they know about the eternal future occupation of those who have not here found life. They bear down with great confidence on this point, the apparent certainty that souls once swallowed up of sin will go on sinning forever, and will only get the deserts of eternal sinning. Such prophecy is a crime, a blasphemy, a deep ungodliness and horrible infidelity. By it, if we venture it, we consent to the going on forever of wickedness, and are really in an attitude to desire that this may be. We deny, also, in this vaticination, the efficient control of God, the infinite persuasion of divine moral government, the just certainties of law and order in the universe. There is no unbelief so deep, so godless, so faithless, so profane and mad, as that which says to the desperate sinner, the outrageous wrong-doer, the hardened wretch, there is no effectual remedy of divine discipline, no ample restoration of injury, no perfect bringing to rights again, no insurance of good against evil *which will be paid.*

SUPREME DEITY IS SUPREME RESPONSIBILITY.

Not only have we been cast on this stream of existence without wish or will of our own, but all the chief conditions of our career have been so far ordered that for nothing whatever can we be held alone responsible. There is no moment of creature existence without the finger of God, no incident or accident of man without the effectual providence of the Divine Father. Neither in creating us with mind, nor in placing us under freedom, has Deity abrogated Godhead, the core of which is living law, and the necessity of which is the living control, the spiritual subjection, of all things that are.

FREE WILL CANNOT BAR GOD'S WILL.

If we do not see how to have this faith in God without a sacrifice of our notion of human freedom, we must make the Christian choice, not the heathen, and keep our faith whatever may become of our notion of free will. It is of no importance that we find out how the Lord works to will and to do; it is only necessary to believe that he does, and to make that belief an integral part of our own devotion to the divine service. No more here than anywhere else is the speculative belief of any value without the practical doing going before and following after; so that even the belief becomes the worst of lies if we make it mean that deity is dead fate, and that we have only to let all go as it will, without care or conscience of ours. It is the intimate union of divine purpose with human, of our working with God's, which Christian faith proclaims to us on the part of the Divine Father, and demands from us as the Father's children. To set free will apart from God, and to make divine will fate irrespective of man, are alike contrary, the one to fidelity, and the other to trust, towards the Father in heaven.

TERTULLIAN AND THE DOGMA OF HELL.

The greatest early master of the dogma of eternal torture of souls was the African Latin Father, Tertullian, whom a candid history of the rise of orthodoxy will show to have been a heathen rhetorician still, in the Christian church, as well as before he was converted. Tertullian, as godfather to the intrusive diabolism of the dogma of hell, has become sufficiently hateful to Mr. Constable, now that his dogmatic motive is changed from damnation which lasts forever to that which burns out by burning everything up. Thus he says of the paternity of the orthodox view, and of its character:

"In Athenagoras, Tatian, and the writer of the spurious works attributed to Clemens Romanus, we have then the earliest known advocates of the theory of eternal life in hell. But this theory required a more powerful advocate than any of the above writers, and it found it somewhat later in the person of Tertullian. A master of the Latin tongue, a powerful reasoner when not led away by his peculiar errors, of a vehement nature and a vivid imagination, he was well suited to impress an idea on an age disposed to accept it, and, spite of his heresies, spite of his strange hallucinations, he left the lasting impression of his mind upon the church of succeeding times. He uses to their utmost possible latitude of meaning most of Plato's terms for the soul. It is, even in the case of the wicked, not subject to death, but must ever continue immortal. It is ever indissoluble, indivisible, an eternal substance, having the very same immortality which belongs to Deity. But it is in the description of the endless agony of the lost that Tertullian surpassed his predecessors, and threw them into the shade. He does not draw any discreet veil over his scene of punishment. Without saying that he took a positive delight in the contemplation of it, he depicts its fancied circumstances with a minuteness and a force that have only been surpassed by the imagination of a Dante, or the agonizing details of a Jesuit or a Redemptorist preacher. Nor can we say that he was wrong, if his theory were but true. No amount of terror, horror, disgust, that could possibly be awakened here in the human mind could be too great, if only by it a single soul could be persuaded to fly in time from this wrath to come. The delicacy that tells us that there is such a hell, but that good manners, or regard for feeling, should lead us to conceal its naked and terrible aspect, is a false delicacy which risks eternity rather than give pain for a moment. Tertullian certainly was not guilty of this false delicacy. He believed in eternal torments, and he drew faithful pictures of them. With him hell was a scene where endless slaughtering *(æterna occisio)* was being enacted, where the pain of dying was to be ever felt, but never the relief which death could bring, for death according to him could not enter into that region of endless life. And God was the author and inflictor of this !"

DIABOLISM OF TERTULLIAN'S DOGMA

Mr. Constable continues :

"Let us look fairly and boldly at this. It was the root, and basis, and *justification* of the theory of Origen. No man can deny that God is able to destroy what He was able to create. No man can deny that God had a power to choose whether He would inflict death upon the sinner or an endless life of agony. Which would He choose—the gentler or the more fearful doom? Will you say the latter ? Why ? There must be a reason. Is it to please Himself? He repudiates wholly this kind of character ! His mode of dealing here contradicts it ; where pain is sharp it is short. Is it to please his angelic or redeemed creation ? They are too like himself to take pleasure in such a course. Did no pity visit the Creator's bosom, they would look up into his face and plead for mercy. Is it to terrify them from sin ? Would it ? What is sin ? Is it not pre-eminently *alienation from God?* What would alienate from Him so completely as the sight or the knowledge of such a hell as Tertullian taught ? Pity, horror, anguish, would invade every celestial breast. Just fancy a criminal with us. He has been a great criminal. Let him be the cruel murderer ; the base destroyer of woman's innocense and honor ; the fiendish trafficker in the market of lust ; the cold-blooded plotter for the widow's or the orphan's inheritance. Let him be the vilest of the vile, on whose head curses loud and deep have been heaped. He is taken by the hand of justice. All rejoice. He is put to death ! No. That is thought too light a punishment by the ruler of the land. He is put into a dungeon ; deprived of all but the necessaries of existence ; tortured by day and by night ; guarded lest his own hand should rid him of a miserable life ; and this is to go on till nature thrusts within the prison bars an irresistible hand, and frees the wretch from his existence. Now what would be the effect upon the community of such a course? The joy at the criminal's overthrow, once universal, would rapidly change into pity, into indignation, into horror, into the wild uprising of an outraged nation to rescue the miserable man from a tyrant, and to hurl the infamous abuser of law and power from his seat. And this is but the faintest image of what a cruel theology would have us to believe of God! Nature steps in, in the one case, and says there shall be an end. Omnipotence in the other puts forth its might to stay all such escapes. *Forever and forever!* Millions of years of torment gone, and yet torment no nearer to its close! Not one, but myriads to suffer thus! Their endless cries! Their ceaseless groans! Their interminable despair! Why Heaven and Earth and Stars in their infinite number— all worlds that roll through the great Creator's space—would raise one universal shout of horror at such a course. Love for God would give way to hatred. Apostacy would no longer be partial but universal. All would stand aloof in irrepressible loathing from the tyrant on the throne, for a worse thing than Manichæism pictured would be seated there —*the One Eternal Principle would be the Principle of Evil.*"

EVIL NOT AN ETERNAL PRINCIPLE.

It does certainly seem a very direct and simple conclusion that if the life of the creatures is only evil it must be because the creator is an eternal Principle of Evil. If that life is in part good, it will be from the life of God in the soul, and this divine cannot but prevail over that human. If there be even *one* dead and damned *soul,* and eternally lost *spirit,* we must see in that single ruin even, that God lacks Godhead, and is himself tainted with evil. If there be no spiritual quick to the creative and sustaining energy, no divinity of eternal life in the power which upholds existence, then is it idle for us to inquire after God.

GODHEAD NOT ABORTIVE.

And so sure as there is the force of deity in whatever beings exist, so sure must it be that this force will strive against sin as long as sin does not yield, and that to this struggle there can be only an end worthy of the power and wisdom of Godhead. Any result other than the cure of evil by the greater divinity of good, would be a root of bitterness and poison of fear to all created being. A hell full of *cinders* even, which is the hope set before us by Mr. Constable's confident and cheerful variation from orthodoxy, would penetrate with horror the very core of creature existence, and deepen fear to hatred, and hatred to madness, as far as ever the thought of such divine abortion should come.

THE CURE OF EVIL ESPECIALLY DIVINE.

The one thing which is divine on earth is the cure of evil—help for fault, deficiency, infirmity, sin and shame, and the one assurance of heaven is infinite help for souls, infinite cure of evil, in the natural force of divinity in the creation. The purest and largest human· sympathy goes increasingly in this direction; this is the leaven, which may be seen pure in the "Our Father" and the commandment of perfect love after the manner of Our Father in Heaven, and which has been a lively presence of divinity in the mass of historical Christianity, long hid, yet effectual to establish under the thick darkness of the world the irrepressible light and life of God with us.

TERTULLIAN'S PICTURE HEATHEN.

The picture which Tertullian drew, of the torment of souls under the consuming preservatives of the divine wrath, was composed by a heathen hand, from heathen colors, and commended to heathen eyes—eyes not yet annointed by the spirit and life which are the grace and truth of Christ. To continue that picture in Christian use to-day, or to permit even the smooch of the faded canvas to offend Christian sight, bespeaks a persistency of tradition, and a weakness of the consciousness of inspiration, which ought not to be.

THE LAST MOMENTS OF HELL.

But the end of this draws very nigh ; the Christian heart is too full of light, too profound in the love of God, too quick with humane justice, and too powerful in tender mercy, to continue respect for the profane and hateful horrors of the old dogma of infernal means to divine ends,—of hell an underlying necessity to heaven. It comes at last to be understood that the Sun of Righteousness indeed has healing in its beams, and that the Infinite Holiness shines with equal grace on just and unjust alike.

HEBREW SCRIPTURE AN ETERNAL EXTINCTION.

The dogma of qualified orthodoxy for which Mr. Constable contends, he first supports by an appeal to the Jewish Scriptures concerning the doctrine of which, on the punishment of the wicked and the particularities of eternal damnation, he remarks as follows:

"We need go no further in order to ascertain the clear, distinct, oft-repeated testimony of the Old Testament. By every unambiguous term it has pointed out the punishment of the wicked as consisting, not in life, but in the loss of life, —not in their continuance in that organized form which constitutes man, but in its dissolution, its resolution into its original parts, its becoming as though it had never been called into existence. While the redeemed are to know a life which has no end, the lost are to be reduced to a death which knows of no awakening for ever and ever. Such is the testimony of the Old Testament."—p. 13.

THE FAITH IS ABOVE HEBREW SCRIPTURE.

It may be presumed, in view of this statement, and of the conflicting orthodox belief, that evident and exact doctrine can with difficulty, if at all, be made out from any Hebrew Scripture references to the subject. But, be this as it may, we must judge any apparent or explicit doctrine by its relation to faith. If it helps us to think that we have eternal life; if it testifies of spirit and truth made evident and powerful for our redemption; if it is profitable for the building of goodly service, and the furnishing of godly ministry ; if by it are brought the deep sanctities of Divine righteousness, and the kingdom of peace from the conflict with evil, then may we know it as divine truth, and ascribe it, but not the earthen vessel which contains it, to the Living Word and Holy Spirit of God. Mr. Constable appeals to Old Testament word merely as such, and with very plain disregard of the analogy of our faith. In this he builds for the fire, not for a refuge of the believing soul.

HEBREW TEACHING, PURELY HUMAN.

It is astonishing that any honest student in our day, knowing the facts in regard to the Hebrew Scriptures, can appeal to them as a sacred canon, or ever use so much as a single text from them, except on the simple ground of its evident and separate truth. Every respectable scholar in Christendom knows that it is Jewish tradition alone which delivers to us the Hebrew writings, and that this tradition is conspicuously human and fallible, from its origin to the present moment.

CHRISTIAN WITNESS TO ETERNAL EXTINCTION.

From the Christian writings—including the New Testament—Mr. Constable draws the following testimony :

"And what did the Christian preacher declare, and the Christian writer write, to that world-wide community which was ruled and bound together, not merely by the power of Roman will, but by the sceptre of the Grecian tongue? In Sermon and Disputation, in Gospel and History and Epistle and Revelation, the propagators of the new religion, asserted of the persons of the wicked—*i. e.* of souls and bodies re-united at the resurrection—that which Plato had denied could happen to any soul. . . . In Jesus Christ was that 'life' which Plato fancied might exist in the soul itself. This life he would bestow upon his people, realizing more than the conception of Plato. But away from Him there was no life. On those who would not come to Him for life there would come finally—after stripes few or many—the end pictured for all by Epicurus. The Gospel brought together the fragments of truth scattered throughout human systems. Those who would soar it raises to God ; those who would revel in the sty of sensuality it sinks to the level of the beasts that perish."—pp. 20, '21.

NO TRUTH OF CHRIST IN IT.

The Gospel of God's sinking of souls to the level of the beasts that perish ! The gospel of compliance with the sty of sensuality, judicial complicity with degredation ! The Gospel of a divine falling back from Christ to Epicurus, from life and immortality disclosed in the creature, to extinction inflicted on the sinful ! It is truly a piecemeal construction of human systems, and no revelation of faith. Drawn where it may be, there is no truth of Christ, no gospel of grace, in it. Is Jesus Christ a bodily enclosure containing all that there is of the living power of Godhead ? Is he not rather a sacrament of infinite grace, a sym-

bol of the power that worketh in us beyond all that
we can ask or even think ?

A STINGY AND SHALLOW CONCEPTION.

Is it some coming in a formal manner, by a motion of assent, or desire, without which no energy
of divinity will so much as stir to help the soul of
the wanderer ? The conception is as stingy in divinity as it is shallow in spirituality. The turning
of the soul to God is no formal act, which now one
has not done and now one has ; it is a life, contin-
uous as being, and permanent as existence. God
does not keep apart in a place for us to look him
up and come to him ; The Divine nature is ever
supernaturally present to human, in an order and
a law of influence, of providence, of redemption.
It is not possible to make any terms of pure faith
speak, as Mr. Constable's statement speaks, of the
separation of man from God. The notion is not
divinity ; it is stark atheism.

ANGLING WITH HEATHEN BAIT.

As for souls and bodies reunited at the resurrection and committed to literal destruction,
with various degrees of torture, the prey of de-
vouring hell, one must angle in the deep waters of
gospel teaching with heathen bait to bring out
even an incidental or accidental word of that sort.

Words enough there may be, on the surface of text and record, which reflect some remaining fragment of the great shadow of darkness which the pure gospel broke up and scattered, but no eye that is single and full of light can possibly read, in any part of the substance of sincere gospel, any such dogma of diabolism.

LUGUBRIOUS MYTHOLOGY.

Mr. Constable does in fact look through Hebrew and heathen mythology to discern the gospel, as the following lugubrious summary of angelic and human fortunes sufficiently indicates :

"Angels fell. No saving hand was stretched from the throne to raise them up. . . . Man fell. . . . How many left behind! How many voices silent! How many pulsations of life stilled forevermore!"—p. 48.

AN ECHO FROM THE FOOL'S HEART.

This is not the voice of Christ ; it is the echo of heathen tradition. The whole pernicious tale of war in heaven, and angels cast out helpless and homeless, has no more to do with Christian faith than any other dark figment of superstition. Equally remote from gospel verity is the fable of a fall of the race. The matter could have no significance if we were able to arrive at some sure knowledge about it ; the gospel does not undertake to investigate the history of our crippling, but to summon us to rise and walk ; and, whether in or out of scripture, speculation about the fall is quite as uncalled for as anything which the record represents as apostolic blunder and folly; Peter's dissimulation, for example, or the carnal ambition of John and James. As for that actual failure of will which is so much in the way of our living to God, it cannot be a matter in which we, or any other moral creatures, are left without help sufficient for our whole need. To say "no saving hand" is to import into theology what the psalmist says that the fool said in his heart. How does the gospel perpetually cry unto all who thus doubt of God, "O ye of little faith ! "

GOD'S EXTINGUISHING WRATH ARGUED.

Mr. Constable further argues, from heathen assumptions, the wrath of God in the extinction of all unbelievers, in the following extraordinary terms :

" 'But,' it might be suggested, 'at least we shall not, if we fall, find ourselves ushered into a doom of which we know little beyond what some faint indistinct fears and misgivings may darkly insinuate.' Yet even such God's dealings with our race show us may be the case. For ages He left the generations of the world *to themselves.* A glimmering tradition, a darkened conscience, nature's indications of a Great Being in whom love, and justice, and judgment, and power had each a place ; these were all myriads had to guide them to the brink of that last step which each one must take for himself, and by himself, into the dark world beyond. We do not affirm or believe of the heathen that all are lost ; but we do know from Scripture that, *as a rule*, their future is without hope. Light enough to condemn, but not enough to save. Light so little as to reduce their guilt to its minimum, but not to make them guiltless ; and yet with this small amount of light and of guilt they endure the second and endless death. And who dares say, with Christ's words in his ears, that none of these lost ones would have heard and hailed to life eternal the words of Christ's Gospel, if they had been addressed to them by the Master or by his disciples. From Sodom and Gomorrha, from Tyre and Sidon, He tells us, souls would have sprung forth to the living call which was heard and unheeded by the callous hearts of Chorazin and Capernaum. But no such call was heard amid the vice of Sodom : no such call mingled with the din of the mariners of Tyre, or with the beating of its waves. They sinned , without law, and they perish without law ; for them it will be more tolerable than for others in the day of judgment, but they will not for all that escape its endless sentence."—p. 49.

SODOM AND CHORAZIN THEOLOGY.

Perhaps we might profitably know more than we do about Tyre and Sidon, Sodom and Gomorrha, and even Chorazin and Capernaum ; or else assume that we know nothing about them with such certainty as to warrant theological inference. It is much safer to argue from the highest view we can rise to of the character of God, and from those undoubted precepts which accord with this view. The Sodom and Chorazin school of theology misapprehends the relative value of obscure human as compared with evident divine facts. It is entirely possible that the story of the former ought to stand aside for the revelation of the latter; and that if we searched the Scriptures for eter-

nal life rather than for odor of brimstone it would
be more to the purpose of humble service to God.

WITH GOD IS NO DARKNESS AT ALL. .

Mr. Constable is quite sure that we know from
Scripture that the future of the heathen is for the
most part without hope ; he does not doubt that
eternity is a "dark world beyond" to average man;
and his eyes discern no companion for the human
soul on the way into that gloomy infinite. So
much comes of not having an eye single to the
revelation of faith, which casts a flood of light on
this subject by simply teaching us to build our
lives on a rule of absolute love to all souls, and our
theology on absolute confidence in the perfect
fatherhood of Deity.

IS THERE A LIMITED SUPPLY OF GOD?

That God emphatically left the generations of
the world *to themselves,* with but a darkened conscience and a glimmering tradition by which to
guide themselves, is an assertion which comes
more by orthodox reasoning than by Christian believing. If there be no Godhead other than that
which appears in the Hebrew and Christian writings, and no care of mankind other than that connected with these writings, it is quite likely that
the supply of spirit and life to the creatures has
been on the stingy scale suggested by Mr. Consta-

ble. But if all that penmen have written and
prophets said be but an earnest of the infinite Living Word and Holy Spirit, we may trust that God
has in no case so shabbily neglected his offspring.
Just light enough not to help, but enough to
make guilty, were incredibly diabolical.

ORTHODOX INTIMACY WITH THE ALMIGHTY.

The elaborate acquaintance of orthodox dogmatists with the divine theory and practice of law is
a curious, as well as a scandalous, negation of that
humility before God which is the Christian basis
of theology. Mr. Constable has found out the
mind of the Lord, ortherwise than by simple trust
and devotion, and he speaks for God as follows :

"We are satisfied that the divine jurisprudence regards
the welfare of the great numbers as its paramount consideration. We see the important bearing of future punishment as it is revealed in Scripture, severe but never unjust,
on this widely stretching interest of unbounded space, of eternal duration. We see how every shade of severity tells on
some vast destiny of the future, from the severity which punishes where the hands had been vainly stretched out all the
day long, and the pleading voice had been mocked at, to the
severity which punishes where no clear voice had ever spok-
en, and where, if such a voice had spoken, it would have
been heard."—p. 50.

SOULS BURNED UP TO MAKE AN EXAMPLE.

If this be true, that God sacrifices individuals to
the mass, and even does not mind visiting with
doom some who would have escaped if they had
clearly understood the way and the necessity, **what**

further is needed to vindicate the atrocious doings
of the persecutor? The practice in the one case
would be no different from that in the other.
Jesuit and Jehovah alike make necessary examples
for the large benefit of the great number. It
may seem very hard on those who suffer at the
stake, and on those who are burned up in hell ;
but then it is useful ! The breadth of this use,
according to Mr. Constable's imagination, is the
grand point. But for diffusing through the universe the impression of one spectacle of souls reduced to cinders for not doing, or for not knowing,
the divine will, Mr. Constable thinks things might
have gone very differently. Thus he says :

" We are by no means prepared to say that if fallen man,
aye, and even fallen angels, had alone been in question, their
treatment by God might not have been widely different. Had
they alone been in question we dare not confine the efforts at
their recovery to those which have been actually made.
Christ might in that case have taken hold of angels, instead
of putting forth redemption only for the sons of Abraham.
Man's day of grace might not in that case have been confined to his life here from the cradle to the grave, but grace
might have followed him on from age to age, and world to
world ere it ceased to strive to win back those who had once
offered to God the pure incense of a creature's praise, who
had once felt the ennobling emotion of the heart's love and
worship of God."

ALMOST PERSUADED TO TRUST GOD.

Evidently, simple faith came near making Mr.
Constable a christian thinker on this subject. How
nearly he comes to feeling constrained to have con-

fidence in the universal and eternal urgency of the
Divine Love ! If he had been, in the humility of
total ignorance, prepared to say nothing at all
about the universe outside of man, and had leaned
to humane rather than heathen justice, and to
'God is Love' rather than to 'Behold Chorazin and
Sodom" what might not have been his hope that
God would not confine his efforts, at future recovery of the lost, to doing nothing at all !

THE PURE HEART AND SINGLE EYE, WHICH TRULY SEE GOD.

It may be assumed that an eye single to the
service of God,—not engaged with distant and dis-
tracting speculation, and not perplexed with anx-
iety to assist the Almighty to maintain the dignities of universal dominion, but rather bent in pure
desire, and holy purpose, and fervent prayer, upon
the simple duties of a humble walk and conversa-
tion, justice, charity and humility, would have
disclosed to Mr. Constable the descent of the .
Divine Word to every lowest depth of creature
existence, and redemption put forth, without respect of persons, on a scale worthy for breadth,
and a scheme worthy for sufficiency and effectual
perfectness, of the alone supreme and blessed God.
It is not given to dogmatists, full of heady opinion,
to gain the vision of peace, in which mortal nature

reads immortal fate, and the troubled clod becomes instinct with the hope of eternal good ; but to simple faith, studying quietness at the feet of Divine Love, it is given to have prophetic expectations of grace following the creature with the persistency and the power of eternity, not lasting beyond fit persuasion, but not resting, forever, until the word of the Lord accomplish that whereto it was sent, and the creature's praise put a crown upon the Creator's perfection.

GOD'S CARE FOR INDIVIDUALS DENIED.

The particular discovery, upon which Mr. Constable has emphatically rested his denial of absolute redemption in the universe, he states in the following confident terms :

"*Mere individual life is not precious in God's sight.* If he scatters it with a prodigal hand, He removes it with a hand that is just as free. In the myriads of human beings reduced in hell to death, in the extinction of the fallen angels, we do but find a particular application of a universal law. Lower creatures know not God, and fade away out of life. Higher intelligences knew Him, turned from Him, made themselves like the beasts, and like beasts are treated. Hell will add its fossil remains to those of the quarries of the earth."— p. 39.

SPIRIT TO SPIRIT, NOT DUST TO DUST.

What does the author of this argument know of the disposition which universal law makes of the living part of the lower creatures ? And how does he know, supposing that the very life of these creatures is extinguished, that man was not made at a higher level of destiny ? Fossil remains are of the form only, not of spirit and life. The only correct comparison would be to say that earth adds her mummies and her urns of human dust to the fossil remains of lower creatures. If these creatures had had souls, and their souls had been damned all to cinders for not knowing and serving God, the fact would afford analogical proof that God may not hesitate to inflict perdition on human souls, alienated through ignorance from his life, and sunk into profound degradation. But as the question is of the fate of spirit and life in man, of the extinction of divinity in the nature of the creature, it will hardly answer to argue from "the beasts that perish." It is not true that moral beings "make themselves like the beasts" by not knowing and serving God ; it is in a figurative sense only that degradation brings down man to the level of the beast ; his spirit remains, if he be indeed born in a higher image, and we are bound to find a destiny for that according to laws of spirit and life, not according to the law of "earth to earth and dust to dust."

MAN CANNOT EXPEL GOD.

And this brings up the point to which the argument for damnation always retreats, that of the supposed power of man to expel good from the very constitution of his being and to adopt evil in its place. Mr. Constable says: " The free creature can defeat Divine goodness for itself. . . The sinner has, no doubt, defeated God's goodness for himself;" and consistently with this he speaks of God's "utter failure to save in unnumbered instances." (p. 52). But this is directly contrary to faith. It is absolute doubt of God. It is faithless unbelief, no matter how we may justify it.

THE DOGMATIC LAST DITCH.

The assertion of free will, or the explanation of it, is of no account whatever in comparison with loyalty to the highest and purest conception of God which has been revealed to us. If we cannot reconcile free will and efficient fatherhood, we can postpone the former matter until by obedience we come to more adequate comprehension. But we can reconcile it if we choose ; it is in dogmatic stubbornness only that sensible men refuse to assume that efficient fatherhood in God is as simple and natural as it is on earth, and as much surer as divine wisdom and power exceed human. There is a criminal perversity in standing desperately in this last ditch, with the absurd claim that man is more than a match for God in the matter of moral. discipline.

MORE ARGUMENT FOR HELL.

It is time to gather into a single quotation what remain of our selected pertinent sentences from Mr. Constable's peculiar argument for hell. They are as follows:

"'Better not to be than to live in misery,' was the judgment of Sophocles, and we ever find the wretched, when suffering has become excessive, calling upon death as a friend. So the close of each agonized life in hell would be longed for here ; would send a thrill of relief through the inhabitants of heaven." p. 3.

"*Their fire is not quenched.* It preys upon them with relentless force. No cries of the. damned arrest it; no prayers ascend from the redeemed for the sin which they know to be eternal death : no feelings of pity in God's bosom interfere to check its course. It burns on, consuming, preying, reducing, until it has consumed and burnt all. When it has spent its force it dies out for want of food, leaving behind it the endless sign of destruction which it has brought on fallen archangel, and angel, and man. *This is the second death.* But we can bear to look upon it *because it is death.* We are not looking upon a picture which would overturn reason and banish peace from all who beheld it. Life has left the realms of the lost. The reprobate felt, but do not continue to feel the consuming flames. These prey upon the dead until dust and ashes cover the floor of the furnace of hell."— p. 34.

" To some this death may be an instantaneous process, a momentary transition from one state to another, like the infant who opens his eyes on this world and then closes them for ever. Here may be the amount of conscious pain for the myriads upon myriads of young and old who, in heathen, and even in Christian countries, from the inevitable moral darkness with which their circumstances had surrounded them, scarce knew wrong from right. To others the process of the second death may be more or less lengthened until we arrive at the case of the greatest human offenders, or that more aggravated one of the spirits who fell from Heaven and drew weaker man along with them in their fall. In our theory we see how it may be, as it certainly will be, more tolerable for some than for others in the day of judgment ; how ;

while stripes many and sore fall on some, on others they may fall so few and so light as scarcely to be felt at all."—p. 37

"*God's ways with the sinner are equal.* They are severe, but they are just. They are full of awe, but they can be contemplated with calmness. They show the award of a justice in whose consequences we can rejoice. Their issue in eternal death, if it brings the sight of sadness, brings also the deep full breathing of infinite relief. We require neither the 'purgatory' of Augustine nor the 'universal restoration' of Origen. Looking on the calmed face of death, we will say, 'it is well.' The woes, the agony, the despair of life are passed away from its features with the sin that produced them."—p. 43.

"He will indeed gather into it all things that offend—all the foul rakings of hate, and pride and falsehood, and selfishness, and lust. But it is with the ominous purpose of Jehu, when he said, 'Gather all the prophets of Baal, and all his priests; let none be wanting,' and 'the house of Baal was full from one end to another.' So will hell enlarge her borders, and the evil of the universe shall descend into it, and fill its wide domain, to be extirpated and blotted out for ever."—p. 66.

"According to their deserving is their chastisement. The time for each one's suffering over, he is wrapped in the slumber of eternal death. Gradually life dies out in that fearful prison until unbroken silence reigns throughout it. They who would not find life have found death. *But the scene remains for ever.* As Sodom and Gomorrha have exhibited to every succeeding generation of men the Divine vengeance upon full-blown iniquity, so will the charred and burnt-out furnace of hell afford its eternal lesson to the intelligences of the future. As angels wing their way from world to world, as the redeemed touch with fresh delight their harps of gold, as new orders of spiritual life are called into being, so the nature and end of sin are always remembered in that scene where so many of the inhabitants of heaven and earth had bid an eternal farewell to the life of God which is so full of joy. That lesson of awe is read and pondered on by all. But it will be a lesson read without the shudder of anguish. They have drunk the waters of Lethe, 'the silent stream,' and forgotten long ago their misery. There is no eternal antagonism of good and evil, no eternal jarring of the notes of praise and wailing; evil has died out, and with it sorrow;

throughout God's world of life all is joy, and peace, and love."—p. 67.

THE ONLY REAL END OF EVIL.

Mr. Constable's idea of the death of sorrow and the end of evil is the selfish and sensual one, not the spiritual and Christian one. It is in the fruition of love, the success of good, the completion of every pure purpose, that Christian faith teaches us to look for final blessedness, while vulgar dogma, following the pattern of heathenism, only asks for the removal of anything painful to saintly sensibilities. On Mr. Constable's theory a mother may twang her golden harp with ever fresh delight after her offspring are entirely burned up, and when she sees nothing but the cinders of them on the floor of the furnace of hell. In Christ, on the contrary, there availeth nothing for her celestial bliss but the fulfilment at last of her maternal love, through the infinite succor of the Divine Order, no covenant of which can ever pass away.

HELL THE FAILURE OF MORAL RULE.

There is no possible manner in which eternal memory of the nature and end of sin, as portrayed by Mr. Constable's theory, could be other than a shadow of irremediable horror to beings decently sensitive to the distinction between good and evil. The " charred and burnt-out furnace of hell"

could only bear eternal witness to imbecile moral
sway in the universe, however much it might tes-
tify of physical omnipotence and the crude vengeance of merely formal law. Happily it is a piti-
ful and beggarly evidence on which Mr. Constable's cheerful hell is promised. If the everlasting
Sodom is as hard to find, and as easy to explain
away, as the legendary cities of the plain, to which
Mr. Constable makes absurd appeal, the scene of
ashes and cinders will prove no more than the picture in a forgotten story.

DIABOLIC DIVINITY.

It is a singular circumstance that a nominal
Christian should suppose himself writing respectable divinity, when he makes "the ominous purpose of Jehu," a vulgar and bloody wretch in Hebrew story, a type of the dealings of the Divine
Father with his children, and represents the Divine Order, not as remedying whatever may go
wrong, but as gathering into everlasting smash
and conflagration a large part of the creation. Such
a diviner may not require either the purgatory of
Augustine or the universal restoration of Origen,
but he does require to understand the first principles of the Christian religion, the sure order of
effectual fatherhood in God, and the perpetuity
forever of fraternal covenant between the children

of God. It certainly ought not to be difficult for a sane mind, decently awake to evident considerations of human feeling, to see the lunatic character of a proposal which should make a mother, we will say, call upon one or two children in this fashion : " Let us be happy now with our harps in the parlor ; Tom, and Jennie and Dick are all burned up in the sitting-room, and father is a heap of ashes in the woodshed." Yet with such infernal toot does Mr. Constable propose to sound the Harvest Home of heaven !

THE MASSACRE OF INNOCENTS.

The nice appointment of preliminary torture promised by Mr. Constable's theory might have a fascination for a Turkish executioner, used to pulling off thumb nails, gouging out eyeballs, pulling joints apart, and otherwise contriving the utmost agonies of slow death. One thing, however, would puzzle the interested Turkish observer of Mr. Constable's scheme, and that is the indiscriminate slaughter of myriads upon myriads of moral infants, persons born and bred under unhappy circumstances, who barely gasp with a first breath of moral life before they find themselves about to be murdered and thrown into the fire. There has never been on earth any monster so brutal in passion, so degraded in character, as to be fully ready to sympathize with such wholesale slaughter of moral innocents. Can it be that the naked atrocity of inflicting eternal capital punishment on " the myriads upon myriads of young and old who, in heathen, and even in Christian countries, from the inevitable moral darkness with which their circumstances had surrounded them, scarce knew wrong from right," should not be perfectly evident to every thoughtful person ? That it is not is distressing proof how little current dogma has to do with real thinking, or with any proper activity of moral feeling.

THE QUESTION OF QUESTIONS.

To conclude this discussion, we will look for a moment at the way in which Mr. Constable is compelled to dispose of the great doctrine of human immortality. His recognition of the prevalence and power of this doctrine is in the following terms :

"Neither a future life, nor judgment and punishment to come, were ideas novel to man. Heathen poetry and prose perpetually discussed them before the preaching of the Gospel."—p. 14.

" Before the preaching of the Gospel the highest order of heathen philosophy had framed for its satisfaction a theory of the immortality of the soul. While far the greater number taught that death was for all, sooner or later, an eternal sleep, there were 'high spirits of old' that strained their eyes to see beyond the clouds of time the dawning of immortality. They framed the idea of an immortality self-existing in the soul itself. Plato, in his 'Phædo,' has given us the marvelous reasoning of Socrates, and Cicero has exhibited the argument in his 'Tusculan Questions.' According to it, the soul is possessed of an inherent immortality. It is of necessity eternal. It could have no end : no death. What was true of one soul was true of all souls alike, whether good or bad. They must live somewhere, be it in Tartarus, Cocytus, Periphlegthon, or the happy abodes of the purified. This sublime philosophical idea passed readily and early into the theology of the Christian Church. We find it running throughout the reasoning of Athenagoras and Tertullian, of Origen and Augustine,"—p. 4.

"'The immortality of the soul was not a question for Jewish and Christian thought alone ; it was the question of questions for the universal human mind. In particular, it was the question of questions in the various schools of Grecian Philosophy. One of the noblest specimens of human reasoning, building its lofty superstructure on uncertain data, that has ever charmed, exalted, and, for our part, we must add, bewildered the human intellect, is found in the dying discourse of Socrates to his friends, handed down to a deathless fame in the 'Phædo' of Plato. Its object was to prove the immortality of the soul—that it could never cease to be—that through whatever changes it might pass, whatever pollutions it might suffer, whatever fearful torments it might endure, there was the deathless principle of the human soul which asserted an eternal life and utterly refused to die. It could never be, according to Plato, a thing of yesterday, an existence of the past but not of the present, a figure once jotted down in the book of life and then blotted out of it for ever. In what terms is the denial of its mortality conveyed ? In the very terms in which the punishment of the wicked is asserted in the New Testament. Where the latter says the soul shall die, Plato says it shall not die; where the latter says it shall be destroyed, Plato says it shall not be destroyed; where the latter says it shall perish and suffer corruption, Plato says it shall not perish and is incorruptible. The phrases are the very same, only that what Plato denies of all souls alike, the New Testament asserts of some of the souls of men. But the discussion of the question was not confined to the school of Plato or to his times. Every school of philosophy took it up, whether to confirm Plato's view, or to deny it, or to heap ridicule upon it. All the phrases we have been discussing from the New Testament had been explained, turned over and over, handled with all the power of the masters of language, presented in every phase, so that of their sense there could be no doubt, nor could there be any one ignorant of their sense before Jesus spoke, or an Evangelist or Apostle wrote. The subject had not died out before the days of Christ. It never could and never will die out. In every city of the Roman world were schools of Grecian thought in the days of the Apostles. In every school the question before us was discussed in the phrases and language of the New Testament."—p. 19.

IMMORTALITY "A MERE FANCY."

Statements such as these are calculated to excite reflection. There is no denial that the question is of supreme significance to the universal human mind, nor that the answer of Plato is one of the noblest conceptions that ever came to the heart of man. It is the marvellous reasoning, the deathlessly famous discourse of Socrates, and the sublime philosophical idea which readily passed into Christian theology, which Mr. Constable proposes to brush aside to suit his theory of hell. He proceeds to the business in the following fashion :

" 'The expression 'immortality of the soul,' so common in theology, is not once found in the Bible from beginning to end. In vain do men, bent on sustaining a human figment, ransack Scripture for some expressions which may be tortured into giving it some apparent countenance."—p. 6.

"At an early period, however, doctrine on this point began to be corrupted, and the corruption grew with a rapid growth. Of all the systems of philosophy in vogue at the time, the most sublime was that of Plato. Of a part of human nature, the soul, it took a very lofty and captivating view. It abandoned the body willingly and forever to its dust, but it ascribed to the soul a life which should have no end.

The reader of Scripture knows how earnestly and frequently Paul warned the Church *against philosophy.* He is the only one of the Apostles who has especially done so, as he was probably the only one of them who had any acquaintance with philosophical systems. In his warnings he does not make any exception. He does not condemn the Stoic or Epicurean schools, and exempt that of Plato, as some of the Fathers expressly affirm of him. He prohibits with all the weight of his authority the introduction of any philosophical system or dogma into the Church. He warned that it would spoil and corrupt, not elevate or strengthen truth.

Many of the early Fathers forgot this warning of the Apostle, and it is among these precisely that we find the origin of error in the Christian Church upon the great doctrine of future punishment. Educated in Platonism, they did not like to renounce it, and flattered themselves that they might, with great advantage to the cause of Christianity, bring at least a portion of their old learning into its service. Some brought less, some more, according as they were more or less thoroughly acquainted with Christianity. But on one point they were substantially agreed. All of them, with Tertullian, adopted in the sense of Plato Plato's sentiment—'*Every soul is immortal.*' On this point Plato took rank, not among prophets and apostles, but above all prophets and apostles. A doctrine which neither Old Testament nor New taught directly or indirectly, nay, which was contrary to a great part of the teaching of both, these Fathers brought in with them into the Church, and thus gave to the old Sage of the Academy a greater authority and a wider influence by far than he had ever attained or ever dreamed of attaining. It was in effect Plato teaching in the Church, under the supposed authority of Christ and his Apostles, doctrine subversive of, and contrary to, the doctrine which they had one and all maintained. This dogma of Plato was made the rigid rule for the interpretation of Scripture. No Scripture, no matter what its language, could be interpreted in a sense inconsistent with Plato's theory. Christ, and Paul, and John, all were forced to Platonise. The deduction of reason, half doubted by Plato himself, was by these Platonising Fathers palmed off on men's minds as the teaching of revelation."—p. 55.

"Connect the immortality of the soul with the Scriptural doctrine of the eternity of punishment, and you inevitably create the dogma of eternal life in misery, *i. e. of Augustine's hell.* Connect it with the other great truth of Scripture, the final extinction of evil and restoration of all things, and you as inevitably create *Origen's Universal Restoration.* For each of these opposing theories there is exactly the same amount of proof, viz: Plato's dogma and a dogma of the Bible ; and, if Plato's dogma could be proved to be a Scriptural doctrine, then by every law of logic Scripture would be found supporting two distinct and absolutely contradictory theories.

"Accordingly, this philosophical idea of Plato is found pervading and influencing the interpretation of Scripture from the second century down to our own day."

In a subsequent chapter we will show the actual influence of this dogma upon the doctrine of the Church leading first to Augustine's fearful theory of everlasting misery, and then, in the revulsion of human thought from this, to Origen's theory of universal restoration. We here merely note the fact that the dogma of the inalienable immortality of the human soul was from a very early period of the Christian Church accepted generally as true.

Now the immortality of the soul, whether as held by Plato, by Origen, or by the Fathers in general, was a mere fancy of the human mind."—p. 5.

THE FOOL'S DENIAL.

The energy and audacity of this denial are worthy of a better cause. 'A mere fancy of the human mind,' says Mr. Constable, of a belief which ranks in significance with belief in the existence of God. If our thought of the dignity of the soul can be summarily snuffed out in this fashion of rude unbelief, the way is wide open to the feet of whoever may choose to say unblushingly that there is no God. It is by the suicide of reason that we take such a step as Mr. Constable is tempted to by a dogmatic necessity. Mr. Constable terribly errs from a wise method of conviction in supposing that he justly degrades the thought of immortality by calling it "the *human* dogma of the immortality of the soul," or "the dogma of Plato, creation of human reason, tradition of men." If the idea were from unregenerate and heathen man, as the false and degrading theory of hell is, there would be justice in stigmatizing it. Mr. Constable's dogma of hell is evidently of the earth earthy, and of the pit infernal, but the idea of immortality, born of the higher reason and purer imagination of man, soars above the deceits of fear and the uncertainties of passion, equally with the thought of God. It is an upward thought, and cannot be made to give way to the base conception of a nature in man no better than that of the beasts that perish, or are supposed to perish. If Mr. Constable chooses to browbeat human faith in the manner of scoffing scepticism, on any point of its ideal anticipations. he should be consistent, and deny at once both the existence of God and the life of God in the soul of man. To sniff at the latter as a mere fancy of the human mind, is no better than to dismiss the former with cheerful contempt. In the one case as in the other, the method is that of naked and abominable unbelief, as repugnant to the Christian consciousness as it is subversive of Christian divinity.

THE SCRIPTURES SEARCHED FOR SUGGESTIONS OF HELL.

The point of relation to scripture teaching from which Mr. Constable takes leave of the two sublimest truths of religion, the immortality of the soul, and the universal restoration of all to good, sufficiently indicates the heathen character of his method. Instead of fastening on such a thought as that of the final extinction of evil and restoration of all things, and working it out to its deepest moral application, the restoration of good in all souls, he attaches himself most closely to the notion of eternity of punishment, and bends everything to the preservation of this scripture pithole, as if the chief desire of his heart were to sniff the smoke of the torment of the damned. It does not seem to occur to him that the doubtful scripture suggestions of hell may be to Christian truth pure and simple as the old dispensation to the new, not meant for everlasting remembrance, but only for terror to men of hard hearts and perverse and froward minds ; or that in any one of a dozen other ways an enlightened faith may learn to rise above this bog of perplexities, the crude doctrine of hell. He considers the logic of texts the rule of faith, when none has been proved more unfruitful and untrustworthy, except for delusion, distraction, and deceit.

PHILOSOPHY MADE AWAY WITH.

It may well be considered necessary to make away with philosophy altogether, not merely with that falsely so called, but with every fruit of reason and product of understanding, to make it at all sure that Christianity will not unfold a clear doctrine of the life of God in the soul of man, an eternal and universal gift from the Creator to his moral creatures. But Mr. Constable's warning is twenty-five hundred years too late to take effect. He should have been on hand with his small cord of concern for damnation to strangle Socrates in his cradle, and to watch with every generation against the birth of sages and saints, to whose illustrious faith has been due so grand a career of the expectation that man shall not prove dust to dust alone, or cinders to cinders, but spirit of Spirit, life of Life, while eternal ages roll.

CHRIST AND ETERNAL LIFE.

The proposal to regard eternal life as "given only through Christ," proceeds upon a totally false conception of Christ, if it is made to mean that we are mortal in soul as well as body until we, by an act of our own, enter into a formal relation to pick themselves up by faith, but that, by the Reason and Spirit of the Divine Father, we have Jesus, and that only those who thus enter into this relation, become capable of immortality. The theory is confused and absurd too to start with. It really should mean that we are mere animals, without a spiritual part, until we earn this, or secure this by the act of faith in Christ; but it actually does mean that the Creator reserves the paternal right to kill off all who do not get an insurance from Christ. In one aspect the doctrine seems to be that we are not endowed with immortality until we get it from Jesus; while in the other it is that we have no right to expect to keep our immortality unless we put it under the protection of Christ. The error either way is in assuming that man has no saving relation to the Reason and Spirit of God, apart from some earthly manifestation of that relation. The handling of the whole matter of the revelation of God to man has been so bunglingly carnal that average divinity does habitually assume that redemption is a matter of our individual relation to an historical Christ, much as if a crop of apples were expected to grow by dead germs picking themselves up from the ground and attaching themselves properly to the living tree. But this is not of Christian faith. The truth in Christ is

not that the blossoms all fell off in Adam, and
living and saving connection with Infinite Being
and Eternal Life, and cannot escape the develop-
ment, discipline, and destiny of living souls. We
are in Christ whether or no, in the divine sense,
and only in the human sense are out of Christ,
until providence and spirit persuade and guide us
to faith and fidelity.

THE REFINER'S FIRE.

The question of hell settles itself the moment
we appreciate our subjection to the moral order of
the universe, and the end of that order to bring us
unto a perfect man. Then we comprehend that
there is no other hell than the furnace of discipline;
that from that torment no wrong-doer can possibly
escape; but that out of it every moral creature
will come a son of God without spot or stain,—AN-
NOINTED OF GOD-WITH-US.

www.ingramcontent.com/pod-product-compliance
Lightning Source LLC
Chambersburg PA
CBHW032157010726
47493CB00008BA/2724